Tal

Presents

Welcome to the September 2008 collection of
Harlequin Presents!

This month, be sure to read favorite author
Penny Jordan's *Virgin for the Billionaire's Taking*,
in which virginal Keira is whisked off to the exotic
world of handsome Jay! Michelle Reid brings you a
fabulous tale of a ruthless Italian's convenient bride
in *The De Santis Marriage*, while Carol Marinelli's
gorgeous tycoon wants revenge on innocent Caitlyn
in *Italian Boss, Ruthless Revenge*. And don't miss
the final story in Carole Mortimer's brilliant trilogy
THE SICILIANS, *The Sicilian's Innocent Mistress!*
Abby Green brings you the society wedding of
the year in *The Kouros Marriage Revenge*, and in
Chantelle Shaw's *At The Sheikh's Bidding*, Erin's life
is changed forever when she discovers her adopted
son is heir to a desert kingdom!

Also this month, new author Heidi Rice delivers a
sizzling, sexy boss in *The Tycoon's Very Personal
Assistant*, and in Ally Blake's *The Magnate's Indecent
Proposal*, an ordinary girl is faced with a millionaire
who's way out of her league. Enjoy!

We'd love to hear what you think about Harlequin
Presents. E-mail us at Presents@hmb.co.uk or join
in the discussions at www.iheartpresents.com and
www.sensationalromance.blogspot.com, where
you'll also find more information about books and
authors!

Kaitie took the phone away from her ear for a second and

Harlequin Presents®

GREEK TYCOONS

They're the men who have everything—
except brides...

Wealth, power, charm—
what else could a heart-stoppingly handsome
tycoon need? In the GREEK TYCOONS
miniseries you have already been introduced to
some gorgeous Greek multimillionaires who are
in need of wives.

Now it's the turn of talented Harlequin Presents
author Abby Green with her sexy romance
The Kouros Marriage Revenge

This tycoon has met his match, and he's decided
he *has* to have her...*whatever* that takes!

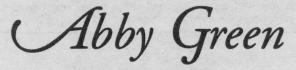

Abby Green

THE KOUROS MARRIAGE REVENGE

GREEK TYCOONS

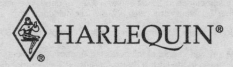

HARLEQUIN®

TORONTO • NEW YORK • LONDON
AMSTERDAM • PARIS • SYDNEY • HAMBURG
STOCKHOLM • ATHENS • TOKYO • MILAN • MADRID
PRAGUE • WARSAW • BUDAPEST • AUCKLAND

ISBN-13: 978-0-373-12759-7
ISBN-10:   0-373-12759-6

THE KOUROS MARRIAGE REVENGE

First North American Publication 2008.

Copyright © 2007 by Abby Green.

www.eHarlequin.com

Printed in U.S.A.

All about the author...
Abby Green

ABBY GREEN deferred doing a social
anthropology degree to work freelance as an
assistant director in the film and TV industry—
which is a social study in itself! Since then it's
been early starts, long hours, mucky fields, ugly
car parks and wet-weather gear—especially
working in Ireland. She has no bona fide
qualifications, but could probably help negotiate
a peace agreement between two warring
countries after years of dealing with recalcitrant
actors.

She discovered a guide to writing romance one
day, and decided to capitalize on her longtime
love for Harlequin romances and attempt to
follow in the footsteps of such authors as
Kate Walker and Penny Jordan.

She's enjoying the excuse to be paid to sit inside,
away from the elements. She lives in Dublin and
hopes that you will enjoy her stories.

You can e-mail her at abbygreen3@yahoo.co.uk.

PROLOGUE

'KALLIE, you have to tell him you love him tonight. If you don't, he'll never know. You're going home in two days, next year you'll be at college or working…this is it, your last chance to tell Alexandros how you feel.'

Kallie's arms were gripped by her older cousin Eleni, her dark face close to Kallie's, her eyes fervent. In some dim part of herself she did wonder at that moment why Eleni cared so much about this. And stifled the thought, feeling mean. Hadn't Eleni been her confidante, having had to listen to her wax lyrical about Alexandros for years on every summer holiday? She was only helping her.

Nerves made her voice shaky. 'But, Eleni, I haven't seen him in ages, he's always in Athens now…' She shivered. *And a little remote.* Which he'd never been before…

Eleni shook her head emphatically. 'Doesn't matter. He's always had a soft spot for you. He's exactly the same, the only difference now is that he's loaded.'

Kallie gulped. *And way more grown up…he's going to laugh at me.*

'Kallie, come on. Don't chicken out now.'

She looked at her cousin. She had that impatient look that always scared Kallie a little.

Kallie nodded jerkily, her heart thumping like crazy. Over

Eleni's head she could see the object of her affections. Alexandros Kouros. Twenty-five years old and so handsome it hurt. Midnight-black hair that shone almost blue-black in the light, curling softly on his collar, a touch too long. His skin a deep olive. His face had a harsh masculinity that made Kallie's insides feel weak. An arresting, utterly captivating quality that drew the eye and kept it there with little effort.

He stood at least six feet four, broad across the shoulders and chest. His body was finely muscled, potently masculine. Sometimes it frightened Kallie, the response she felt around him. Like it was something she couldn't control, didn't fully understand…

They were in his palatial family villa, which was right beside her grandmother's in the hills above Athens, where she always spent her summer holidays. Every year, the end-of-summer party in the Kouros villa was the highlight of the social scene. Kouros Shipping was one of the biggest companies in the world. And since his father's untimely death two years before, Alexandros had taken full control without even breaking sweat.

'Kallie, he's never going to see you as anything but a friend unless you go and take things further.'

'I know.' Kallie was anguished, her attention brought back into the room, to the events that her cousin seemed to be determined to set in motion. She'd never done anything so bold in all her life, usually preferring to hide behind a book or in the hammock at the end of her grandmother's garden, dreaming. She didn't even know if she really wanted to do it. Suddenly she saw Alexandros across the room take a bottle of something off a table and disappear. Eleni had followed her gaze. She turned Kallie to face her.

'This is it, Kall—now or never. You'll regret it for ever if you don't. By the time you see him again he'll be married with three kids…'

The thought made Kallie feel physically ill…or maybe

that was the wine Eleni had been plying her with to get her courage up. Eleni held up the glass again. Kallie shook her head, as it was it was already swimming slightly. The sight of it made her feel nauseous. It was the first time she'd drunk anything alcoholic and she really wasn't sure she liked it.

'Go, Kallie. *Now.*'

Fuelled by something bigger than her—the wine, the sense of finality about everything—Kallie moved forward as if in a dream, through the crowd in the room, out the door that Alexandros had disappeared through and onto the patio. The warm air washed over her, bringing her to her senses somewhat. She almost turned around and went back inside, but saw Eleni at the door. No going back.

She didn't see Alexandros at first—he was hidden by an overhanging tree that trailed its leaves along the stones of the grand patio. Then she saw him, his tall lean body, jacket off, leaning against the wall, and it made something inside her flutter to life. She moved forward. Thoughts swirled around her head, like a drumbeat…a mantra…as she approached him.

It's now or never. If I don't do it then I'll never know, he'll never know how I feel…

She held her breath and stepped into the space where the tree formed a kind of hidden clearing. The faint sounds of the party drifted out on the breeze but Kallie was oblivious to that. Her heart nearly jumped out of her chest it was beating so hard. Alexandros had his back to her but she could see that he had a bottle in his hand and was lifting it up, drinking from it. She must have made a noise because he whirled around, the bottle clenched in one hand.

'Who's that?' He peered into the gloom and Kallie stepped forward slightly. 'Kallie? Is that you?'

She stepped forward. 'It's me.'

He turned away. 'You should go back inside to the others.'

She was stung at his obvious desire to be alone. His dismissal. She realised a little belatedly that he'd been in a strange mood all evening, dark, brooding, as if a black cloud clung to him. And it seemed even more apparent now.

Having come this far, she ignored him and kept walking till she was almost beside him, the twinkling vista of Athens laid out below them at the end of the garden. Her heart was beating so rapidly she felt light-headed.

'I'd like to stay, if that's all right.'

He shrugged and took another swig from the bottle. Kallie grabbed it from him, taking him off guard, and took a drink herself before he could stop her. She coughed and spluttered as the liquid burnt her throat. He stood up straight and clapped her back, sitting her back on the low wall beside him. A wry grin on his face.

'What were you expecting? Wine?'

Tears streamed down Kallie's face, shocking her out of her nerves for a moment. 'What *was* that?'

'Ouzo.'

She shivered suddenly when she realised that they were close together, his muscular thigh burningly close to hers.

He reached for his coat and draped it over her shoulders. She had to fight not to give in to the sensation, not to close her eyes and breathe his scent deeply. They sat in silence for long minutes, neither one moving. That brooding energy emanated from Alexandros. The air seemed to grow thick around them, tension mounting, and Kallie wondered feverishly what to say, how to break it. But Alexandros turned to her suddenly.

'Kallie…why did you come out here? You should go back, it's getting dark.'

She looked at him, hurt in her eyes. 'I just…I don't mind just sitting here with you…'

He groaned softly and ran hands through his hair. 'Sorry. I'm just…not the best company tonight.'

She laid a hand on his arm, and looked at him. 'Do you want to talk about it?'

He looked at her for a long time with an intensity that made something coil deep in Kallie's abdomen, something alien and tight...*hot*. He seemed to be fighting some inner battle, struggling with something. Then it passed. She held her breath as he reached out a hand and caught a lock of her hair, letting it slide through his fingers.

'Your colouring is amazing, do you know that?'

Kallie grimaced, felt like squirming under his gaze. 'It's horrible. I burn too easily. I blush too easily.'

And I'm too fat...

Every insecurity rose up all too easily.

He shook his head. 'No, you've got your mother's colouring. A typical English rose...'

'That's why my father says he fell in love with her.'

Something dark crossed his face and he let her hair go. The moment was gone. And in that same moment she knew she didn't have the guts to do this. She should leave Alexandros alone. To fight whatever demons were chasing him.

'I'll go...'

She got up to leave and promptly stumbled when the ground swayed as she stood up. Alexandros's arms came out automatically, swinging her into his chest to regain balance. Her wish to leave dissolved in a flash of heat. His chest was against her hands, strong and broad and warm, his heart beating steadily. His scent surrounded her. She looked up into those dark, fathomless depths and was lost, no more capable of moving than hiding the blatant desire in her expressive eyes. She was in a bubble of sensation so acute that she'd lost all sense of reality, space and time.

She lifted a tentative hand and with one trembling finger traced the outline of Alexandros's mouth, the hard sensual contours. She could feel his breath against her palm.

'Kallie…what are you doing?'

Her eyes jumped up to his and for the first time in her life she felt bold, filled with some unknown, unexplored feminine power. Not knowing how she had the nerve, she just said simply, 'This…'

And she reached up, closed her eyes and pressed soft, warm lips against his.

For a long moment he didn't do anything. Kallie felt something move through her, an aching *wanting*. It stunned her with its intensity. And then hope sprang in her breast. He wasn't pushing her away. Would he kiss her back? She wanted him to, so much. Her lips moved tentatively against his…and then abruptly her world erupted and tilted. Alexandros stood and pushed her away from him with two harsh hands so quickly that Kallie was dizzy and would have staggered back except for his unwitting support. His jacket fell to the ground behind her.

'What the hell do you think you're doing?'

He let go and somehow Kallie managed to keep standing. She could feel a tide of red heat climb her chest, her body throbbing painfully with all the newly discovered sensations clamouring for release.

The way Alexandros was looking at her, with such disdain, disbelief and *horror*, made her turn to jelly.

Her voice was hesitant. 'I…I was kissing you.'

He was scathing. 'I know that, Kallie, I'm not stupid.'

Mortification twisted her insides. 'I'm sorry… I don't know what…' She shook her head and stumbled away a little.

He caught her back with his hands on her shoulders. 'No, Kallie, what the hell was that? Why would you try and kiss me?'

'Because…' She looked at him, backlit by the falling dusk. So handsome. And it made something burn in her belly, dissolving her embarrassment. She had to tell him.

Now. 'I did it because…' she swallowed painfully '…I love you, Alexandros.'

He straightened, his whole body taut, bristling. 'You *what?*'

'I…love you.'

Nothing moved. Kallie saw Alexandros looking at her and the blatant shock on his face changed to confusion and then something else…disgust.

He took his hands off her shoulders suddenly as though he'd been burnt.

'Look, I don't know what you're up to, Kallie, but I don't appreciate it. I'm announcing my engagement tonight and if someone had seen… *Hell.* Just go, Kallie.'

His words dropped into her brain but didn't register. Engagement? Married? To whom?

Kallie felt a mad desire to burst into hysterical laughter and then just as suddenly felt very silly. And very small and very young. Like a child caught playing dress-up, her face smeared with make-up. Acutely conscious all of a sudden of her not exactly svelte figure and her dress, which she'd borrowed from Eleni, hoping to be more grown up, and which was a little too tight.

Her lips felt stiff and numb. Her body cold.

'I'm sorry, Alexandros, just forget this…all of it. Forget it happened, forget *me.*' She whirled away and ran, down the steps, into the garden, away from the patio, away from everything. She heard him call after her once but she didn't stop, and he didn't follow.

The tears came as she ran and when she finally stopped she hunched down and cried and cried until she could hardly see. She cried for being so naïve, so silly and for listening to Eleni. She must have been emboldened by some lunar magic or madness, the wine… As if someone like Alexandros Kouros would *ever* notice someone like her, would ever even want to kiss someone like her. She cringed when she thought of how she'd thrown herself at him. He'd as good as had to pry her hands off him. She wiped her cheeks. One thing was for sure, she was *never* going to touch alcohol again if it had led her to do something so stupid and ill-judged.

Miserable, Kallie went back up towards the house, unable to avoid going around it to return home. And as she passed the open patio doors, she couldn't help but look inside. The room was hushed, the designer-clad, jewel-bedecked crowd with glasses high in the air as they toasted the newly announced union of Alexandros and the stunning woman at his side. His fiancée. Pia Kyriapolous, the famous model. They looked so beautiful together Kallie's eyes watered again.

She felt a tap on her shoulder and whirled around, very aware of her tearstained cheeks. Eleni. Looking at her with sympathy written all over her face.

'Oh, Kallie, I'm so sorry…'

Something in the way she said it made Kallie very still. Her stomach churned as she suddenly remembered her cousin's words. *By the time you see him again he'll be married with three kids.* 'Please, tell me you didn't know about this, Eleni.'

Eleni looked defiant. 'I did you a favour, Kallie. If you'd known, would you have gone near him?'

Of course not!

She lashed herself again at her phenomenal naïvety and knew it was in that moment that something in her died, or grew up.

She pulled away, physically and mentally, curled up somewhere inside herself. Something in Eleni's face made her want to protect herself. It was something she'd never seen before. *Or noticed.* She contrived to toss her head, exactly how she'd seen her cousin do it a thousand times, usually when Alexandros was around, and shrugged. 'It's no big deal, Eleni. I can hardly compete with Pia, now, can I?' She even managed a small laugh from somewhere. 'But, like you said, at least I tried…*ne?*'

And for the first time in her young life, she summoned all the adult poise she could, and swept away, leaving the party, her cousin and Alexandros behind.

When Kallie woke up the next morning, the tight ache in her chest didn't seem to have dissipated one bit and she had the horrible sensation of thinking it could have all been a bad dream, but of course it hadn't. Her only consolation was that she knew Alexandros would probably be in Athens, and that she was due to go back to England the next day. She prayed Alexandros would stay in Athens till she was gone. And that no one would ever know what had happened. Except them. And Eleni. Who at least, Kallie thought with a shudder of relief, hadn't witnessed her humiliating efforts.

However, she came downstairs to noise and confusion and commotion, Her parents and Alexandros in the middle of it all. Her father was shouting at him, thrusting a newspaper in his face.

'How could you? We trusted you. She's seventeen, for God's sake. Little more than a child. Isn't it enough that you're getting married to one of the most beautiful women in Athens? You had to mess around with Kallie.'

They didn't see her come down the stairs behind Alexandros. His voice came low and blistering. 'Pia's family have surprisingly little regard for their daughter marrying someone splashed across the middle pages of the biggest tabloid in the country. They also have surprisingly little regard for her marrying someone who, and I quote, "never wanted to follow his father into business." Thanks to your daughter, my engagement is off as of today.'

Her mother, who hadn't seen her either, stepped forward at that moment and slapped Alexandros across the face. Kallie saw his head jerk back. In the shock of silence afterwards, her mother's voice was shaking with emotion as she said, 'Surely you *know* she's always had a crush on you? You were like a son to us.'

Kallie's legs stopped. They wouldn't work and she felt herself going icy cold and clammy, an awful sick feeling in her stomach. She must have made some kind of noise because they all turned and saw her.

She couldn't believe what she'd just witnessed, *the violence,* and how her mother had just laid out her innermost feelings for all to see. Alexandros grabbed the paper out of her father's hands. The anger and disgust on his face made her want to turn around and run away. She saw the livid red hand imprint on his cheek.

'*You—*'

Her father cut him off. 'Kouros, get out of this house. You are not welcome here, now or ever again.'

Alexandros turned away from Kallie and back to her father. 'Believe me, I don't want to see any of you again. Especially *her.*' He flicked her a look that was so contemptuous that Kallie took a step back. And then he was leaving, walking away, out the door.

Acting on pure impulse, Kallie ran after him, ignoring her parents' calls to come back. Alexandros's long legs nearly had him at the gate that separated their neighbouring properties.

'Wait, Alexandros…wait!'

He stopped so suddenly that she almost ran into his back. He turned and gripped her arms with hard hands, his face close to hers. And suddenly he didn't even look angry any more, he looked sad. And that was even more confusing. Her head swam as she tried to understand what could have happened.

'I thought we were friends, Kallie. Why did you do it? You've ruined everything…and all because I didn't want you?' He shook his head. 'You were the one person who didn't seem to expect anything from me. I trusted you and you set me up, blabbed everything.'

What was he talking about?

'I don't know what—'

He shook his head, cutting her off with a fierce look in his eyes, his lip curling in distaste. An image came back into his head of her reaching up to kiss him with a bold look in her eyes. One thing he knew now, without a shadow of a doubt, was that he'd never really known Kallie Demarchis. Just like he'd never really known any of them. Kallie's family had been like a second family to him and yet they could throw him out of their lives, their house. He'd been a fool to trust them. *To think he'd thought her innocent, untainted... sweet!*

'These last two years you've really grown up, Kallie, haven't you? Become just like the others. You heard about the engagement and thought you could have a go, too? Try to get in there?'

His face was so harsh that Kallie didn't know how she still stood in front of him. And he wasn't finished. 'Seventeen is just a little too young for my tastes, though, and you don't have what I need.'

He shoved the newspaper at her. 'Oh, and next time you want to do a kiss and tell? If you're trying to keep your identity a secret, it's a good idea not to submit the copy from your own e-mail address. You're nothing but a spoilt little bitch, Kallie, and not even a particularly bright one.'

She watched as he disappeared from view, her mouth open...words stuck in her throat. *Her e-mail? Kiss and tell?* As if in an awful sick nightmare, she looked at the paper which had fallen at her feet. It lay open on a very bad-quality, grainy black-and-white photo. As if taken with a camera phone. But one person was unmistakable. Alexandros. The golden boy of the shipping world. And the woman with her arms wrapped around his neck, straining against him, was most certainly *not* Pia Kyriapolous. The girl in the picture would be unidentifiable to any but those who knew her well, and was far too chubby to be the well-known model. A screaming headline. THE GROOM! THE NIGHT HIS ENGAGEMENT IS ANNOUNCED...!

CHAPTER ONE

Seven years later, The Ritz Hotel, Paris

ALEXANDROS KOUROS was bored. It was like a heavy mantle around his shoulders. A black cloud that spread outwards from his very depths, pervading everything. He was oblivious to the fact that he was surrounded by opulence. The opulence that came with being one of the wealthiest men in the world, in one of the world's most exclusive hotels. Hushed whispers encircled him. He tuned them out, the superlatives bouncing off him. They'd surrounded him for years, but he'd never courted them, never needed any assurance.

So handsome...so young! The most successful shipping magnate since Onassis... Even more money... Most eligible bachelor...

Now the constant murmurs that followed him wherever he went only added to the ennui he felt. He'd achieved a pinnacle of success attained by just a very few, and only imagined by most. And it had been hard won, which should make it all the more sweet. But was this it? How could he be feeling like this when everything he'd ever worked for lay at his fingertips, when he could snap those fingers and influence the world's economy with just a word, a command... And if this wasn't what he wanted, then what the hell was? A distant memory, an old faded dream, reared its head. *That* had long turned to dust.

A touch on his arm, not gentle. It was predatory, possessive and brought his attention back to the room. To the woman at his side. She was considered one of the most beautiful, desirable women in the world…and she was the latest in a long line of similar women who had graced his arm, his bed.

'Darling…'

He felt irritation prickle across his skin. Unfortunately, for the sake of politeness, he couldn't remain oblivious to her. He turned to face her and smiled tightly, taking in the platinum blonde of her hair that suddenly looked too garish, too bright. Took in the heavily made-up face, the hard, avaricious glitter in her eyes. The diamonds flashing around her neck. Diamonds that he had bought with scant regard to their worth. He made a split-second decision, suddenly aware that he didn't find her at all attractive any more. Had he ever?

Isabelle Zolanz didn't know it yet, but she was on her way out. He felt relieved for the first time in weeks. The thrill of knowing he'd be free again already helped to diminish the crushing boredom. He didn't want to spend another minute with her. In fact, he decided there and then that they would leave, he'd take her home, break it off now. His suit felt constrictive and he had to school his features into some semblance of neutrality.

Just as he was about to open his mouth and speak, to say some platitude, something flashed in the corner of his eye and he turned on a reflex to look. The room was packed, and in the doorway on the other side of the room stood a woman. She'd obviously just arrived, craning her neck looking for someone, standing on tiptoe. For a split second the noise in the room faded. He couldn't take his eyes off her. Goosebumps broke out on his skin. The hubbub rushed back.

She was utterly captivating. But in a way that he couldn't

define, in a way that confounded him. Not model gorgeous. Not preened or buffed. But something about her caught his attention. She was only of average height but was perfectly proportioned, his expert eye assessing in seconds the way her curves dipped in and out in all the right places. A little more voluptuous than he'd normally go for but calling to him on some deep, primitive level. The simple black V-neck dress drew the eye to her waist and the slopes of her breasts. A pendant hung around her neck, the gem resting in her cleavage. It sparkled as the light hit it and he dimly recognised where the flash had come from.

Just as he also recognised with shock that he felt a compelling desire to walk over, take her hand and lead her back outside to see for himself if her skin was as soft and silky as it looked. The urge was so strong that he actually felt his feet shift, his whole body turn, as if to move in her direction. He wanted to touch the place where her gem rested. And he had to admit with sudden chagrin, as possessiveness was an alien emotion to him, that he wanted to lead her away from the other men who he could see already taking note of her arrival, too. She was like a breath of fresh air in a musty room.

She was pale. Her face had clear, clean lines, cheekbones clearly delineated, eyes wide apart and almond-shaped, making him want to see them up close, see their colour. Honey-streaked hair hung in loose waves over her shoulders and a heavy fringe, swept to one side, hid and alternately revealed tantalising glimpses of her eyes.

His hooded eyes followed her as she walked with effortless feminine grace, her hips swaying, the inward curving line of the small of her back and the jut of her rounded bottom making Alexandros feel a twinge of reaction in his trousers. More than a twinge, in fact.

He felt a tug on his arm and almost shook off the hand that rested there, still completely engrossed in watching this woman. And only remembered then where he was, who he was with. He felt shocked. For a moment he had become entranced. Forgotten nearly everything. He shook his head mentally. Definitely a sign that he needed to move on, if he was lusting after a complete stranger across a crowded room.

But there was *something* about her. Something he couldn't put his finger on, some kind of familiarity, as if he knew her or had seen her somewhere before…

He tore his gaze away with more of an effort than he liked to admit and looked down at Isabelle again. A smooth smile was in place as he remembered wanting to leave, her harsh beauty even more jarring now after *that.*

He murmured, 'Forgive me…I have an important early meeting tomorrow. Would you mind if we left?'

'Not at all, darling. I'll get my coat from the cloakroom.'

She squeezed his arm and smiled, clearly anticipating, somewhat misguidedly, that he wanted them to be alone, and walked away.

As he watched her walk away, Alexandros felt no compunction, no guilt at what he was about to do. A woman like Isabelle Zolanz was well versed in the way he worked, and men like him. He had no doubt she'd be put out, but as no emotions were invested, he knew it'd be for the loss of his money, his largesse and the social standing that came with being seen on his arm. It was a state of affairs he was used to. He enjoyed the thrill of the chase. But lately, if he was honest, every conquest had become stale…flat. And there was invariably very little chasing involved.

Even so, he conversely felt the relief flood him again and unconsciously sought out the other woman. But she had disappeared. He grimaced slightly. It was probably for the best. He knew all too well that seeing something like that, building up an image, no matter how beautiful the woman—*and she wasn't even that beautiful!*—always led to disappointment.

They were all the same. All the ones that hovered around him like bees around a honey pot. In the rarefied circles he moved in, he didn't encounter another type. Sex and money. They were the two currencies that he understood and knew all too well. He played the game like a virtuoso. In bed and out of it.

A cloud crossed his mind. Was he ready to be free again? There was a certain amount of protection to be had in keeping a mistress. A respite from the tiresome attempts of other women to get his attention. And then he was forced to remember something. He scowled. He actually did need a woman right now. He needed a lot more than that and it irked him beyond belief. But even as he saw Isabelle in the distance, collecting her coat, his stomach felt acidic. He certainly wouldn't be asking her.

Kallie pushed her way through the crowd. She craned her neck looking for her uncle and finally spotted him in a far corner. When she reached him she kissed him on the cheek. 'Sorry, Alexei, I got held up at work.'

'No matter, my dear. Let me get you a drink.'

He spoke quickly and seemed a little jumpy to Kallie. Which was reinforced when he grabbed a glass of water from a passing tray and practically shoved it at her. He avoided her gaze, looking distractedly over her head as he did so, and Kallie felt an uneasy sense of foreboding. Her uncle looked almost…nervous.

'Alexei…'

He suddenly jostled her behind a plant and screened her from the room with his body.

'*Alexei…?*' Kallie's voice was indignant. She knew her uncle was given to dramatics but this was ridiculous. He was acting as if they were in a bad spy movie. 'What on earth is wrong with you?' She smiled widely and then whispered *sotto voce* in his ear, 'Are we hiding from your mistress?'

He turned back to face her, affronted, 'Kallie Demarchis, you know I would never look at another woman.'

She put her hand on his arm, soothing him. 'I'm teasing…but you're acting so strangely. Do you think I can come out from behind this plant?'

He paled for a second as he took in something across the room. Kallie frowned and couldn't hide a spike of fear. 'What is it? You're scaring me now.'

He looked back at her and loosened his collar. 'Kallie… it's someone…someone is here, someone you haven't seen in a long time…someone…'

'Who?' she asked, beginning to feel a little exasperated.

Her uncle avoided the question. 'I tried to call you on your mobile just now but they wouldn't let me use it…then I got waylaid by someone else and couldn't stop you coming in…before…'

She tried to be reasonable, patient. 'Before what? Alexei, why wouldn't you want me to come in?'

She could see her uncle gulp visibly. 'Because…well, because…Alexandros Kouros is here…'

Alexandros Kouros…

The noise in the room became a buzzing sound in Kallie's ears. She was vaguely aware of her uncle practically wringing his hands and very dimly, in a far-away place, his words slowly sank in with the same devastation as the *Titanic* hitting the iceberg. She felt an icy numbness take over her limbs and would have dropped her glass except that her uncle caught it in time. The water slopped onto her dress. At least it's only water, she thought with banal shock, it won't stain.

Alexandros Kouros…

It was just a name, she rationalised somewhere within her still buzzing head. Just a name, attached to someone very famous. Well known. Very wealthy. Very handsome. Influential. Someone who didn't even enter her sphere or orbit. But yet…it was the name of someone infinitely memorable. Intimately tied into her past, who had once been in her orbit— *had been her orbit*—as big a part of her past as if he'd been one of her own family.

Someone she'd never dreamed of having to face again. And now he was here, *somewhere,* possibly even just mere feet away. Panic gripped her, making her skin clammy.

Her uncle had grasped her hands and was looking at her. She forced stricken eyes to his, her face leached of all colour.

'Kallie, darling…I'm so sorry. The thing is, you can't be here… If he sees you…'

She nodded slowly, not even really sure why she was nodding, only seizing on the words "if he sees you". She didn't even want to imagine for one second what that reaction might be like…or what *he* might be like now, in the flesh.

She was more than dismayed that she couldn't be feeling just a mild curiosity, to be able to shrug it off, declare the fact that he was in the same room as a funny coincidence, uncaring whether or not they bumped into each other. She was stunned by the strength of her own reaction after all this time, the well of emotion that was still so close to the surface. It shook her to the core and scared the life out of her. She'd never guessed it was still there.

It had only been a kiss, for God's sake, little more than a kiss. Yet it had led to so much more. She chided herself that he must have moved on from what had happened…but then she had to remember with a sudden upsurge of nausea that *she* and her stupid actions had been instrumental in the calling off of his engagement…the ruination of the so-called marriage of the decade. To the woman he loved… How would he have possibly forgotten that?

Her uncle was getting more agitated, looking slightly shifty. 'The thing is, Kallie…I didn't tell you before now as I knew it might upset you, but I've started doing business with him again. Since your parents died, that is. Obviously your father wouldn't have approved but, you see, I *had* to, Kallie. I had no one else to turn to and when he gave me an appointment…' He laughed a sudden brief laugh, sounding like a little boy. '*Me!* An appointment. It would appear he's willing to let bygones be bygones, with me at least. Now, if it had been your father, that would have been a different story—' He seemed to catch himself, realising he was starting to babble, and gripped Kallie's hands tighter. 'But if he sees *you*…'

The familiar clench of grief at the mention of her parents went unnoticed for once. Her uncle was referring, of course, to the scandal that had gripped Greece for weeks. The press had devoured the story of how Alexandros Kouros had taken advantage of his family friend's young daughter. Just when he was about to become engaged to Pia Kyriapolous. And even though Kallie had cried tears of frustration, trying to defend him, no one had listened, too intent to paint him the villain and her the poor innocent victim.

It had been even more futile trying to assert her own innocence with regard to the photo and story, and only recently had she confirmed for herself who the real culprit was. The story had since faded, of course, and since her grandmother's death the summer after that, Kallie had only been back to Greece a couple of times. She'd never seen him again.

Her uncle looked so comically terrified that it brought her back to reality. Kallie's heart went out to him. No doubt he was watching his entire business float down the river if Alexandros Kouros took one look at her and decided to wreak belated revenge.

'Alexei, I don't care if you're doing business with him…really. Look, I'll go. Believe me, I have as little desire to see him as he must have to see me.' *Liar. You'd love to see how he's turned out…*

Her heart beat a staccato just at the thought. A whole

Pandora's chest was being opened and Kallie was helpless to stop it. This was too close a call and she had to get out, get away. She kissed her uncle on the cheek and squeezed his hand. 'I'll call you tomorrow, we can talk more then.'

He nodded with obvious relief and Kallie walked away quickly, head down, not looking left or right, just focusing on getting through the crowd in front of her. She comforted herself with the thought that even if he did see her, she'd changed a lot in seven years, and she would come so far below the radar of his usual women that he'd be unlikely to recognise her straight off, thus giving her time to escape.

Almost at the door, she had to duck out of the way of a waitress carrying a loaded tray and she careened into someone's back. They twisted to look around and Kallie was horribly, familiarly aware of someone very tall, very broad, with black hair curling on his collar. The back of her neck prickled and afterwards she wondered at how she hadn't had a stronger sensation, a stronger warning of imminent danger. Quite the opposite, it seemed, some evil force had directed her straight into the lion's jaws. She couldn't move. She was rooted to the spot. Unable to flee the danger.

CHAPTER TWO

SHE looked up…and up again. And her eyes met all too familiar dark, fathomless depths. In a heart-stoppingly handsome face. A face she knew well, because it had stayed vivid in her consciousness. Her mouth, which had opened automatically to apologise, stayed open.

'Alexandros Kouros…' She wasn't even aware of saying his name out loud. It was as if she had to say it to make it real or to pray that he was a figment of her imagination. But he was no figment of anyone's imagination. He was too vital… too dark…too big and too…gorgeous. *Why* did she have to bump into him? It was too cruel.

'Do we know each—?' He stopped and turned fully. Black brows pulled together, frowning.

It was her! The woman… But he knew her…

His eyes raked her up and down. They both knew that the way she had said his name had been more than just the banal recognition of someone famous.

Kallie, while praying he *wouldn't* recognise her, was conversely stung somewhere very vulnerable when he clearly had no idea who she was. She forced her stricken limbs to move, to try and get away. She couldn't believe her awful luck. Why hadn't she just stayed where she was? Why hadn't she taken more notice of where she was going? Why was he looking at her like that? She had to get away.

'Sorry…'

She turned and just when she thought she could let her breath out, when she'd taken a couple of steps, her arm was taken in a punishing grip. His deep voice rang with stunned incredulity.

'Kallie Demarchis?'

She closed her eyes. The worst thing had just happened. Her breath came back but it was painful. She longed to be able to keep going, to walk away. The burning humiliation was still so vivid that she had to open her eyes again to halt the images rushing through her mind. His grip was painful on her arm and yet it lit tiny fires that raced up and down over her skin. She finally turned, with little choice to do anything else.

She turned, hitched her chin and looked up. 'Yes.'

His face was unreadable, but she saw something flare in the depths of his dark eyes. Anger. Shock and anger. He moved his intense gaze from hers and looked her up and down, slowly and thoroughly.

'Well, well, well. Little Kallie Demarchis. All grown up.'

He spoke almost musingly, as if to himself. 'Your eyes give you away. They're such a distinctive colour. Blue and green. Only for that, I don't think I would have recognised you. You must have had work done. If I remember, you always were insecure…but it's definitely been worth it.'

It was only when his eyes insolently dropped to her breasts that Kallie gasped with outrage, welcoming it because it crashed through the numbing shock. She finally managed to tear her arm out from his grip. 'How dare you? I've done no such thing. I'm sorry I bumped into you, believe me, but I'm sure you'll be only too happy to excuse me.'

'Don't you mean you're sorry for wrecking my engage-ment all those years ago…or sorry for dragging my name through the tabloids…or sorry for publicly humiliating me, for getting me thrown out of your house like a common thief?'

So much for hoping, or even praying that he might have forgotten…

Two spots of colour burned in her cheeks and her eyes flashed. Alexandros had to suck in a breath against his will.

She was magnificent…and how had she transported him back to a time he had believed he'd forgotten for good, so easily and so quickly?

He reeled. Reeled with the shock of coming face to face with the very woman who'd captivated him across the room. Reeled with the force of her beauty up close. And now reeled with the knowledge that it was *Kallie Demarchis.* The girl who had taken petty spite and used it to almost ruin him. He looked down at her. Except now she wasn't a girl. She was a woman. A very sexy woman. A woman who was making the blood hum in his veins and an arrow of desire shoot straight to his groin. An instant chemical reaction.

Kallie had opened her mouth again to speak, but before she could do, a blonde vision appeared beside Alexandros, a scarlet-tipped hand on his arm. A blatant indication of ownership. And who could blame her? Kallie thought fuzzily, closing her mouth, words dying unsaid. Even without studying him—*she didn't have to*—he was the most handsome man in the room, head and shoulders above all other men. A perfect, potent specimen of manhood, sexual energy radiating off him in waves that she fancied were almost visible to the eye.

He'd been a gorgeous young man but now…he was quite simply devastating. The years had filled out his frame, had added maturity to his face, the lines starker, harder but no less beautiful. He now had an edge of sexual charisma that came only with age, confidence and experience. His hair still had the curls of his youth though, and that made something poignant erupt in Kallie's chest. The other woman's slightly, delightfully accented tones broke through Kallie's reverie.

'Darling…aren't you going to introduce me?'

Alexandros couldn't stop staring at Kallie. Again. He'd been mesmerised *again*. To the exclusion of everything else. He could see Kallie flounder, too. As if they'd both forgotten they were in a public place, surrounded by people. But Isabelle had to be attended to. Kallie cut in, though, before he could speak. She looked apologetically at Isabelle, cutting out Alexandros.

'Please, excuse me. I have to catch someone before they leave. It was…nice to see you again, Alexandros.'

And she was gone, had melted into the crowd. All he could see was her shining head every now and then as it bobbed and weaved away from him. The urge to snatch her back was strong. Very strong. And the gnawing, clawing feeling of boredom that Alexandros had felt earlier was gone. As though he'd just been injected with vital energy. And desire. The kind of desire he hadn't felt in a long, long time. The fierce elemental kind that made his insides burn for completion, for fulfilment.

Reluctantly responding to Isabelle's urging to go, he was already making plans in his head. Plans that didn't involve her, but that did involve Kallie. He couldn't believe how she'd strayed into his path, like a plump, succulent piece of fruit.

He hadn't thought about her in years—*hadn't had the time*—and only fleetingly had she crossed his mind when her uncle had approached him recently. Agreeing to meet with her uncle, he'd congratulated himself that he'd left all that behind…*until now*.

Kallie Demarchis.

He couldn't stop repeating her name in his head.

He'd seen her uncle earlier, and had acknowledged him briefly across the room, but who would have known that she'd have come there, too? Who would have known that she'd be the very woman who was stoking the dying embers of his desire? And who would have known that he'd ever get the chance to do something about her petty, spiteful act all those years ago? An act with ripple effects that had vastly eclipsed the actual incident involved. She'd never been made accountable for those actions. The feelings of betrayal and anger from those days surprised him now with their resurgence, with their freshness. He didn't like being reduced to such primitive emotions.

The initial anger that had gripped him fed his energy. Seeing Kallie again tonight, the timing was so perfect that he almost laughed out loud. The linkages that existed in place for him to take advantage of this opportunity were mind-blowing with their simplicity. If there was such a thing as karma, this was it. And he was going to enjoy every minute of it. And enjoy every piece of her.

Two days later, Kallie stared at the blinking light on the intercom of her phone. Her PA's disembodied yet unmistakably awe-struck voice floated through again. 'Kallie…did you hear me? Alexandros Kouros is on line one for you.'

Just like that. Alexandros Kouros is on line one…

Her heart, which had stopped, started to beat again, slowly. She'd somehow, in the past forty-eight hours, tried to convince herself that she hadn't actually seen him. That it had been some sort of bad dream. She tried to speak but nothing came out and with a huge effort she shook herself out of the inertia that seemed to have taken control of her every limb. 'Thank you, Cécile. I'll take it now.'

She picked up the phone, pressed the button under the blinking light and took a deep breath.

'Hello?'

'Kallie.' The deep authoritative voice sounded close in her ear and made her sit up straight.

'Alexandros.' She marvelled that she could sound so cool when her head and insides seemed to be self-combusting. The treacherous unfurling of desire that had started the minute she'd seen him again was still there. And that knowledge scared her. What did he want? Kallie swivelled around in her chair and didn't take in the view of Paris outside her third-floor window, the Eiffel Tower going unnoticed in the distance. Her voice was clipped, tense.

'What can I do for you, Alexandros? I'm sure this isn't a social call.'

Even if they didn't share history, the most successful Greek shipping magnate in the world wouldn't be ringing up her small Anglo-French PR firm.

His slightly accented tones came like silk down the phone into her ear again. 'It was certainly a shock to see you the other night. It's been, what, six years?'

'Seven.' She had answered far too quickly and easily. Her hand tightened around the phone, hoping that he hadn't noticed. He didn't seem to as he spoke again. And took the wind out of her sails.

'I was sorry to hear about your parents…'

Kallie was feeling more and more bemused. This man had been thrown out of their house by her father. Slapped by her mother. He had told her he never wanted to see her again. He must have picked up something in the silence because he said, 'Despite the past, Kallie, I *was* sorry to hear of their deaths.'

The shock at hearing his voice was beginning to wear off. 'Well…thank you.'

She repeated her question again. 'What…what can I do for you, Alexandros?'

He didn't speak for a long moment, and she was almost about to repeat her question when he said with devastating banality, 'I want you to have dinner with me tonight.'

Kallie took the phone away from her ear for a second and

looked at it. Alexandros was up to something. That was one thing she was sure of. She existed on his list of people to call for dinner somewhere alongside Attila the Hun. He whizzed around the world on his private jet, doing billion-dollar deals, meeting heads of state and dating what seemed to be an endless stream of models and actresses, like Isabelle Zolanz. It was only afterwards, when she'd got away from him, that she'd realised who the other woman had been: a famous French actress. He certainly didn't ring people he despised to ask them out for dinner. People who had ruined his chance for marital happiness. And even by some accounts a huge merger with his fiancée's family shipping company, but she wasn't sure about that. She'd avoided listening to anyone talk about it at the time and in England, at least, it hadn't hit the news with the same force.

'Somehow I don't think you do, Alexandros.'

'But I do, Kallie. I'd like us to catch up,' he returned easily. Far too easily. As if he'd anticipated exactly how she'd respond.

Kallie's hand tightened even more on the phone and she felt dizzy. This had to be some kind of bad dream, a sick joke. He was playing with her.

'Alexandros, I don't want to go out for dinner. You said you never wanted to see me again.'

'Well, I've changed my mind.'

'Why?' she almost pleaded.

'Let's just say you owe me at least this, don't you think?'

Kallie closed her eyes weakly. What could she say? She searched frantically for an excuse but, as if reading her mind, his voice trickled down the line like dark honey, weaving around her senses.

'I had a nice chat with your assistant. She was most helpful in informing me how clear your diary is this evening.'

Kallie cursed Cécile mentally. And yet she couldn't stop the entirely uncontrollable part of her that was intrigued…that wanted to be able to say yes. She had no excuse not to, and to fight was to invite him further into a dialogue that might take them down a path she didn't want to go.

Her voice was stiff with obvious reluctance. 'It would seem that I have no choice. I'm finished work around six this evening…when would suit you?'

'I have a table booked for dinner at the Hotel de Crillon at the Place de la Concorde. Eight o'clock. I can pick you up…or send my driver?'

Kallie thought of her tiny flat in the Marais district and spoke quickly. 'No. There's no need. I can meet you there.'

She could almost feel him shrug on the other end of the phone. 'As you wish. Eight, then. I'll wait for you in the bar.'

CHAPTER THREE

ALEXANDROS put down the phone and stood up from the leather chair. In custom-made Italian trousers and shirt, he walked over to the window of his office and stuck his hands deep in his pockets. The action drew the fabric taut over his buttocks, the shirt stretched over broad shoulders. He cut an impressive, very masculine figure silhouetted against the window. He thought back to the other night. The remnants of the shock of seeing Kallie again still lingered. Along with the shock of how much she'd changed, and the desire that had pounded through his entire body. That still pounded through it just from hearing her voice.

It had been harder to extricate himself from Isabelle than he had thought. It had taken two nights. More jewellery. And dinner in the newest, most expensive restaurant. She'd been more tenacious than he'd realised and he was relieved the episode was over. She'd begun to fancy herself as perhaps being in line for marriage and had not been pleased to discover that, instead, he'd wanted to end things.

He looked out at the horizon, his gaze skipping absently over the Eiffel tower in the distance. His thoughts centred on Kallie. Her blue-green eyes flashed again in his mind's eye. Seven years might as well have been seven seconds. He'd been transported back in time that quickly. Felt all the old emotions surge up. Emotions he'd long thought he had under control. Apparently not.

He'd been such a fool all those years ago. How had he missed seeing her true colours? How had he ever thought for a second of her family being closer to him than even his own? His hand clenched into a fist as he remembered how vindictive she'd been. And how he hadn't seen it coming at all.

He'd been fooled into somehow believing that she of all people wouldn't have changed. He could still remember seeing her across the room that night, smiling sweetly at him. It had been like balm to his ravaged spirit. A cool reminder of happier times, more carefree concerns. And *then* to have her morph into some kind of temptress, right in front of his eyes. He could still feel the astonishment that had slammed into him. So immobilising that he hadn't even pulled away from her kiss immediately.

Everyone along the way had shown their true colours in the end. Not least his own family. But for Kallie to join those ranks…and to behave in a way that he would never have even imagined. She'd had him thrown out of her house, his fiancée's life, and his name had been dragged through the mud.

By using her own e-mail to send the photo and story, it had been so obvious she'd meant it like a taunt! And she'd had the nerve to reveal deeply personal details to the newspaper that only she could have known…because she had been the only person he'd ever told them to. Details like wishes and dreams…aspirations that had had nothing to do with what had been expected of him.

His mouth slashed into a grim line. The vultures who had already smelt a possible weakness on his father's death had circled for a long time. He repressed a shudder. And they'd nearly got him.

He had to acknowledge that when he'd told her those things he'd been two years younger, before his father had died, and she'd been fifteen. He hadn't yet been flung at top speed into a reality that had torn any rose-tinted dreams away. A reality that had mocked him for having been so open. The fact that she would have stored those conversations up to use in such a way made his stomach turn.

That period had been the turning point for so much. A turning point that meant he'd never, ever let anyone get that close again. He operated on his own now. He didn't need anyone.

He slammed a fist against the wall beside him. *How* could she have changed so much in those two years? He closed his eyes. He'd asked himself the questions over and over. The fact was, he'd been betrayed. All he'd ever represented to anyone around him had been a means to make money. To generate wealth. When he'd turned his back on her that day, he'd turned his back on a lot of things.

Enough. Kallie Demarchis was about to learn what it meant to cross Alexandros Kouros. It was time for her to taste a little of the reality he'd had to taste.

His mind went to the plans he'd set in motion since seeing her again. It was true that he'd never been one with a lust for revenge, seeing it only as a device that could betray a weakness to the opposition. That could betray emotion. When all around him had descended to that visceral level in business, he never had. And it was part of the secret of his success. Part of what had helped him claw back control, get to the top. Go further than even his father had done.

He thought of how, when Alexei Demarchis had come to him for help, he'd debated for a long time whether or not to entertain the man. He smiled grimly. He'd made the right decision. Fate had just told him so.

Now he was willing to rethink his views on revenge… especially when it was laid out for him so enticingly, so temptingly, when his loins ached with a hunger that was all too rare. It was time for him to lay the ghost to rest and indulge a little.

* * *

Kallie took in the passing streets of Paris. She'd never normally take a taxi, the métro being more than efficient for her needs, but a last-minute crisis at work and a derailed train had meant she was under pressure to make the Hotel de Crillon for eight. She felt nervous and jittery. Her hands felt clammy, so she smoothed them distractedly on her dress. What would it be like, seeing Alexandros again? He was even more handsome than she could have imagined. The stark, masculine lines of his face were indelibly imprinted onto her retina. He'd seemed even bigger to her. Six feet four of nothing but lean, hard muscle. Her belly clenched in a pure spasm of sheer, unadulterated lust and she tried to take her mind off his physical attractions.

He hadn't ever married, there had been no talk of it since the debacle with Pia Kyriapolous. He obviously hadn't managed to mend bridges there. From what Kallie could remember, Pia had quite quickly married someone else. No doubt further rubbing salt into Alexandros's wound. Pia had been one of the most successful models in Greece, the daughter of another very wealthy shipping magnate. The day after the engagement had been announced, Kallie had had to endure everyone saying that it was a match made in heaven.

Kallie knew now with maturity and hindsight that her developing sexuality had been hopelessly snared by Alexandros. But, of course, he hadn't noticed that. Hadn't noticed *her* like that. So that's why, with the very vocal, almost bullying encouragement of Eleni, she'd gone out to find him that night. She closed her eyes and gulped. She did *not* need to go there now, not when she was going to be seeing him in mere minutes. She was a grown woman, in control of herself and her emotions.

She smiled grimly to herself, opening her eyes. She'd confused immature, infatuated lust with love. And as for Eleni… Kallie sighed deeply. There was no point thinking about that now, there was nothing she could do anyway. It was all water under the bridge.

She saw that the taxi was pulling into the area outside the main door of the hotel. She went hot and then cold in the space of seconds. They came to a halt. The porter stepped forward to help her out. She looked up at the distinctive name on the awning over the door and, with her legs feeling decidedly wobbly in her high heels, stepped into the distinctively honey-coloured marble foyer.

At the door to the small bar she saw him immediately. And felt the urge to turn around and step back outside. Go home, pack up and move back to London. She straightened her spine and walked forward. He was sitting on a high stool, a glass with dark liquid swirling around the bottom in his hands. He didn't see her approach and there was something so intense about the way he was studying the liquid…almost as though he was looking for some kind of answer. Kallie dismissed her fanciful notions and came to a halt near him, doing her best not to be bowled over by his physicality.

She cursed her voice, which sounded unbearably husky. 'Alexandros…'

He looked up and those dark, deep depths caught her and sucked her in. She was in trouble. He stood with lithe grace, no hint of expression on his face. He reached to take her coat. Reluctantly she let him help her out of it, studiously avoiding touching him anywhere.

'Sorry I'm a bit late. I got held up at work.'

He smiled. It didn't reach his eyes. 'No problem. We'll have a drink here and then go through.'

He was charm and urbanity incarnate. And he didn't fool her for a second. Kallie followed him on legs which had become like cotton wool. He led her over to a table and gestured for her to sit down. She was glad of her simple silk shirt and plain back skirt. Glad she hadn't made an effort. The waiter arrived and Kallie ordered water.

Alexandros lifted a brow and ordered a whiskey for himself. 'No alcohol tonight, Kallie?'

An immediate blush stained her cheeks as the meaning of his loaded question cut through her. He was referring to *that* night, the way she'd grabbed the bottle from his hand. Again she was aghast at his memory. Had he forgotten nothing? She shook her head tightly.

She wasn't going to tell him that ever since that night she'd never touched a drop of alcohol. She'd had plenty of opportunity but somehow, when it came to it, she just couldn't. Something would flash back into her head, and she'd find that even the smell turned her stomach. She had the very uncomfortable suspicion that her bizarre reaction was somehow tied in to the fear that something out of her control would happen. Like it had that night.

'Look, I'm sure you're busy. We really don't have to do this whole dinner thing. Do you want to just tell me—?'

'All in good time, Kallie.' He bent forward and Kallie fought against arching back into the chair. She felt very keenly as though she were involved in something huge, but something she had no clue about. Like a fly caught in a web. And she didn't like it. Not when Alexandros smiled at her like the hungry spider.

'Tell me,' he asked equably when her water arrived, 'how have you ended up here in Paris? Didn't you go to college in the UK?'

She nodded slowly, determined not to show her fear, her sense of being intimidated. But despite her wariness, she found it surprisingly easy to talk.

'After my mother and father died, I wanted to get away from London. I've always loved Paris. I had spent a year here during my business degree, taking French…' She shrugged, awkward under his intense gaze. 'It seemed like an obvious choice. I had money from my inheritance and set up our small firm. We got busy quickly as we seemed to corner the niche in doing PR for English companies setting up here and vice versa for French ones in London…'

Alexandros thought of the rapid research he'd done on Kallie that day. The countless pictures he'd unearthed of her at various parties, looking like the life and soul of each one. Although her appearance opposite him begged to differ, as she sat there in her plain skirt and blouse, which did little to disguise the curves he'd seen on display the other night.

And despite her abstinence from alcohol so far, he didn't doubt that she used *it* and maybe more to enhance her partying. He felt inarticulate rage start to rise, some indefinable sense of disappointment, and forced himself to be civil. For now.

'You've done more than corner the niche. I read about your company in the financial press—you were awarded best new small business last year. That's some achievement.'

Kallie was too surprised at his praise and it was given in far too much of a backhand manner for her to feel a glow of pride. She shrugged again modestly. 'Like I said, we just got in at a good time. Britain has never been so close to France with the tunnel, and plenty of people are capitalising on it. I'm one of many.'

'Yes, but not everyone makes a success of it. You obviously have the Demarchis genes.'

'Which are nothing compared to the Kouros genes,' she pointed out with a wry smile, feeling herself start to relax slightly. The smile surprised her and she pursed her lips immediately. She knew that to feel relaxed was entering very dangerous territory.

'Maybe so.' Alexandros's eyes dropped to her mouth and rested on her full bottom lip. Her sudden smile had caught him off guard. His head felt uncharacteristically hazy as all he could imagine was how it might feel to take that bottom lip between his, explore its lush cushiony softness, parting them softly with his tongue…

With relief, he saw the head waiter from the restaurant approach the table. 'Mr Kouros, I'm sorry to bother you. Will you be having another drink here or taking your table now?'

He stood with the grace of a huge jungle cat, making Kallie shiver. 'Now, Pierre. Thank you for waiting.'

He waited for Kallie to stand and precede him from the bar, curling his hands into fists when an urge struck him to reach out and place a hand on the curve of her hip, feel it sway against his hand, explore how the silky fabric of her shirt played across her skin. He took in the sheen of glossy hair, longer at the back than he'd thought, the soft waves tamed from the unruly curls of her youth.

The crippling ennui was definitely fading, and he had to admit that he was looking forward to the future for the first time in a very long time.

'Good?' Alexandros's soft question came across the table. Kallie looked at him warily. He lounged back in his own chair. At obvious ease in the sumptuous, gilded surroundings, the famous restaurant, Les Ambassadeurs. She'd heard that this was the hotel that hosted every year an exclusive ball for debutantes, where twenty-four privileged young women from all over the world, aged from fifteen to nineteen, would have their introduction into society. Kallie's insides clenched when she thought of herself at seventeen.

She dragged her attention back, nodded and set her knife and fork on her cleared plate. A slight flush of colour entered her cheeks. Why couldn't she have just ignored the plate of food? He must be disgusted by the way she'd tucked in. Stress for her meant eating more, not less, and she hated to be reminded of the fact. It wasn't so long ago that she'd still carried around her puppy fat.

'Amazing,' she said tightly with a bright smile. 'My appetite has never been a problem, as I'm sure you remember.'

His eyes ran down her body, what he could see of it. To where her waist curved in before swelling out again to her hips in a way that was fast becoming a provocative invitation to him.

Kallie felt her insides heat up under his look. Why had she drawn attention to herself? She remembered his nasty jibe that she must have had work done. His eyes thankfully rose to meet hers again.

'You seem to still be self-conscious. You were a little chubby maybe, but what teenager doesn't go through that?'

Chubby…!

Humiliation flooded Kallie when she thought of how impassioned she'd been that night on the patio. How her body had burned for him, how for once she'd been unaware of anything other than the sensations that had overwhelmed her, her untutored, gauche advances. And how she'd ever imagined for a second that he might be turned on by her. But, of course, he hadn't been. It hadn't taken long for him to come to his senses. She wanted to close her eyes, block out the potent sight of him.

'Alexandros, surely it's time to tell me—'

He ignored her plea, butting in. 'No. It's not.'

She flinched back slightly at his harsh tone and he seemed to notice. She could see a pulse flicker at his jaw, as if he was controlling something.

'Tell me, Kallie. Why did you feel it necessary to tell that rag about our conversations? Wasn't it enough to just publish the photo?'

She flushed a dull red. It had killed her when she'd found out just how her own trust had been abused so abominably. But by then it had been too late. And would he understand what it was like to be a teenage girl in the throes of young passion? How she'd merely confided in someone she'd thought she could trust? Of course he wouldn't. The Alexandros she'd known a long time ago might have…but this man wouldn't.

She gave thanks for having held her tongue about Eleni…for not having blurted out the truth. Eleni's situation meant that Kallie couldn't use her as an easy excuse for vindication. She had to find out just what he wanted. Because *that* was as clear as the nose on her face. He wanted something.

Kallie hardened her heart. She had to. Those conversations he mentioned had belonged to another time, a more innocent time when she'd believed he'd had different sensibilities, like her own. But, she had to remind herself, once his father had died and he'd taken over running Kouros Shipping, he'd changed. Under his hands it had gone from million-dollar profits to generating billions. That wasn't the same person she'd known who had confided a wish to go to art college. He'd obviously smelt the chance to make money, lots of it, and he'd changed.

But, pathetically, she couldn't stand the thought that he would tar her with the same brush, despite the evidence she knew was stacked against her. 'I didn't… It wasn't how you think…' she said ineffectually, miserably.

He leant forward, his face hard. 'Oh, and just how was it, Kallie?'

Now they were getting to it. Kallie felt something like relief flood through her. This she could handle. Alexandros being angry, hating her.

She looked at him slightly defiantly. She could, at least for the moment, be honest about this. 'I never intended to hurt you, Alexandros. Believe what you want—you made up your mind that day.'

He was derisive. 'Oh, you didn't hurt me, Kallie. But you did wreak a trail of destruction with your careless, cruel actions.'

She swallowed painfully. She hadn't been intentionally cruel. But he was right—she'd been careless, and foolish. She couldn't argue with him about that.

'Your uncle Alexei…'

He didn't finish the sentence. His rapid changes of subject caught her off guard. He was like an opponent conducting some form of mental martial art. Immediately she was wary. She clenched her hands into fists under the table.

'What about him?'

Alexandros shrugged negligently. 'I hear he's having some difficulties…'

Guilt flooded Kallie. She suddenly remembered her uncle's words from the other night, how he'd mentioned he'd *had* to get in touch with Alexandros. It hadn't occurred to her to question him, she'd been so distracted.

'What kind of difficulties?' she bit out. Hating Alexandros with passion at that moment. He was milking every single moment of this dinner. Her nerves were on a knife edge of sensation so acute that she thought she might break in two.

'The kind that would be solved with a cash injection of a few million euros.'

Kallie tried not to let shock show on her face. She had a sudden very acute fear that they could be vulnerable to Alexandros, who was clearly out for some kind of revenge now.

'You don't even have your shares, do you?'

How did he know that?

She shook her head warily.

'Apparently you couldn't even wait until your parents were cold in the grave before you cashed them in…'

She gasped at the cruelty of his words. It had been nothing like that. She'd handed them over to Alexei and *he'd* cashed them in, giving her the small amount she'd needed to set up her business. She hadn't wanted anything else to do with them and her uncle had needed them.

She leant forward, unaware of how it gave Alexandros a tantalising view of her cleavage beneath her shirt. She quivered with rage and injustice.

'What I did or didn't do with my shares is none of your business, Alexandros.'

He shrugged like he didn't much care and Kallie felt impotent, wanted to walk around and slap the look of smug superiority off his face. It held all the arrogance of his forebears.

'The fact of the matter is that your uncle has come to me for help…for a loan, if you will.'

Kallie sagged back against her chair. *Oh, Alexei, what have you done?* Her uncle had never been the brains behind Demarchis Shipping. That had been her father, until… Her mind slammed down on painful memories.

'Look, Alexandros, what do you want? Surely…surely this can't be because of what happened all those years ago?'

'Why not, Kallie? Do you think that what you did wasn't so bad after all? That time might have diminished it? You tried to seduce me and when it didn't go your way, in a fit of spoilt pique you lashed out. You singlehandedly stopped a marriage from taking place—'

'But, Alexandros.' Panic was making her insides liquefy. 'Surely Pia would have given you the benefit of the doubt, let you explain? I'm sure you could have convinced her that it meant nothing, was nothing…' she had to stop for a second when her heart clenched in remembered pain '…if she loved you…'

Her remark caught him on the raw, caught him in a place he'd shut off long ago.

'You're priceless. *Love?* It was never about love, Kallie, it was a business arrangement. A merger between two families. Needless to say the merger never happened as soon as they lost faith in my ability to do the job. Thanks to your revealing titbits…' The rage rose up again. '*Theos,* Kallie…'

She was speechless. She'd always assumed that he had loved Pia. And even though she hadn't leaked the kiss-and-tell story to the paper, and had had nothing to do with the damning photo, she'd always felt guilty for trying to seduce Alexandros when he'd only wanted to be friends.

Her vulnerability and pathetic weakness for this man *still* made her blood boil. She opened her mouth, about to proclaim her innocence, and stopped. Eleni. And it wasn't just Eleni. Even *if* he knew, Kallie was still in her own way responsible, too. She couldn't say a thing…angrily impotent at the way she was trapped, she put down her napkin and went to stand but he reached across the table and caught her hand.

The feel of her smooth warm skin, the frantic pulse beating like a trapped bird, called to Alexandros, scrambled his brain for a second. He had to fight for control and remember what he was there to do.

'I'm not finished with you, Kallie. In fact, we haven't even started.'

She pulled her hand away, uncaring if people were looking. 'There's nothing starting here, Alexandros. I'm leaving.'

His voice was low and lethal. 'No. You're not. If you stand up, so help me, I will pick you up and carry you out of here over my shoulder. Don't think that I won't. So we can do this here and now, or we can cause a furore of interest, give the paparazzi outside something to photograph and do it back in my apartment.'

She had been in the act of standing and sat down again slowly. She knew without a doubt that she didn't want to be alone with him and that he wouldn't hesitate to do exactly what he'd said.

When she had sat back down he continued agreeably, as though discussing the weather. 'As I was saying, your uncle is in need of a substantial loan. A loan to keep Demarchis Shipping afloat…literally. This puts me in an interesting position, wouldn't you say?' He didn't wait for her answer. 'I was quite prepared to do business with Alexei, as it suits my needs, too, but *now* things are intriguingly different. Needless to say, it won't make the slightest bit of difference to me should I choose not to help him. But it would make all the difference in the world to him…and your family.'

The lines in his face were unbearably harsh and Kallie quailed at how time and circumstances had turned this man into such a lethal combination of sheer ruthlessness and icy cool. And at the part she had unwittingly played.

He continued unflinchingly, 'He's a tough old dog, but he's exhausted every other avenue and, as he told me himself, I'm his last hope…'

Kallie was stung with guilt that she hadn't known, that her uncle hadn't confided in her. That she could somehow be instrumental in potentially doing damage to her family hurt her unbearably. Yet still, even through this, she was so aware of Alexandros across the table that she felt dizzy with his presence.

'How have they not told me—I mean, how is this possible?'

She suddenly looked very young and lost and alone to Alexandros. Her eyes were huge, shimmering, blue and green. And he felt something twist in his chest before he ruthlessly quashed it back down.

'Who knows? By selling your shares so promptly, by coming here to Paris, moving away from the UK—your mother's own home, and your father's adopted home—perhaps Alexei and your family thought you were taking a stand away from them, weren't interested in their problems.'

It killed her that he could deduce this, but she hadn't. And the familiar wave of grief washed through her. She lifted pain-filled eyes to his, speaking without thinking. 'It wasn't like that. It just became too much. After the funeral, the business was all they could talk about. All they ever talked about. My father had as good as taken his own life, and my mother's with him and no one wanted to talk about that. It was Demarchis Shipping this, Demarchis Shipping that…' She broke off when her voice caught and she desperately blinked back the sting of tears, hating that he might see any hint of vulnerability.

She strenuously fought to hide the brightness from his narrowed gaze and only looked back when she felt more under control. He had an intense look on his face. And then it was gone. Replaced with that implacability again. She hardened her own jaw.

The emotion that had softened her features could have been a figment of Alexandros's imagination and he felt himself flounder slightly. This wasn't going exactly how he'd imagined it. He wanted to reach over and run the pad of his thumb across her cheeks, down to her lips…cup her delicate jaw. He was fast losing the thread of why they were there. All he wanted was to stop talking and take her to bed. Spread her underneath him. The speed with which this woman had taken over his senses shocked him.

Kallie felt anger boil up at the unfairness of it all. All she had done had been to bare her heart and soul to this man. And he had crushed that into the dust. *Before* the story had even erupted. She jabbed a finger towards him. 'Look, Alexandros, I can't undo the past any more than you can, with all your money. And I wasn't alone out there that night. I may have… initiated things. I tried to tell my parents, to explain…but they wouldn't listen.'

He held up a hand, derision on his face. 'Please. It's a bit late to try and tell me that you defended my honour when you cold-bloodedly arranged for the photo and the breathless story in the papers—that shows a level of premeditation on a par with the most corrupt politician. But…' he silenced her protest with a look '…there is one way that Alexei need never know about this, one way that I will give him his loan, help him out of this situation he's become embroiled in.'

She flushed at yet another indication of how much he knew

and focused on how she could avert a disaster within her family. 'How's that?'

'You, Kallie.'

And then before his words could sink into her head, which felt like it might explode, he asked her abruptly, 'Do you remember my uncle Dimitri?'

She nodded, her brain still scrambled, trying to make sense of everything.

'He died a month ago.'

'I didn't hear that he was unwell. I'm sorry,' she said stiffly, wondering where this was going.

He shrugged, his face closed, belying the fact that he had loved Dimitri like a father. Something he would have credited Kallie with knowing…once.

'It was sudden.' His black gaze fixed on Kallie. 'It's part of the reason I've asked you here.'

Along with the burning desire that holds you in a grip so tight you have to shift in your seat every two seconds.

A pulse beat at his temple.

Kallie's face felt rigid. She couldn't help the sarcastic response. 'Well, I was wondering… You were hardly calling to reminisce about old times.'

Shut up, Kallie!

He didn't seem to notice her self-flagellating turmoil. The waiter appeared, removing their plates. Kallie refused dessert, ordering a coffee, Alexandros asked for a liqueur. He waited until his drink arrived before fixing her with that intense gaze again. He wasn't going to make this easy. Kallie's full armour was erected against him.

'I have to admit that bumping into you was a shock…but also perfect timing, a certain kind of serendipity, if you will.'

She looked at him warily. 'Timing, for what exactly?'

He looked at her across the table. He clenched his jaw and refused to let his gaze drop to that shadowy line of her cleavage, the gem on the end of that same pendant swaying back and forth, kissing her skin. Skin that looked soft and... He clenched his jaw even harder and focused with effort.

Think of what you need. Focus on business. This is business. And revenge... Nothing else.

Alexandros valiantly concentrated on that and not on Kallie's all too grown-up charms. There'd be time for that later, he vowed.

'I need a convenient wife, and *you*, Kallie, I've decided, are going to oblige me.'

Kallie looked at him dumbly, shock washing through her body.

CHAPTER FOUR

'I'M SORRY?'

'You should be, Kallie. It's time to start atoning for what you did seven years ago. I bet you never thought it would catch up with you. I have to admit, I hadn't planned on doing anything, I was quite happy to settle for never crossing your path again, but bumping into you the other night, together with a slightly…' His mouth twisted as he looked for words. 'Unfortunate set of circumstances that I'm in, has all been very fortuitous.'

A nightmare. She had to be stuck in some kind of nightmare. This couldn't be real. Kallie's mind disengaged from everything. She looked around dumbly and could see couples dining. Lovers holding hands. Men having business dinners. They looked real. And then everything seemed to rush back into focus. Someone was calling her name.

'Here, drink this.'

Alexandros was reaching across the table with dark amber liquid in a glass. His after-dinner drink. She shook her head violently and pushed his hand back, snatching hers away abruptly when she felt the strong bones of his wrist.

He looked at her, his voice unbearably harsh. 'What's wrong with you?'

She shook her head, ignoring his question. 'Why on earth do you want to marry me, Alexandros?' She waved a jerky hand that still tingled from the contact with his. 'Why would you want to do that?'

He put down his glass, smiled grimly. 'Don't worry, Kallie, I don't *want* to marry you. When my uncle Dimitri died, he left me his share of Kouros Shipping. It's the last piece not in my control.'

She looked at him blankly. Still in shock.

'It was expected. He'd always made it clear where his inheritance would go.'

She nodded vaguely, incapable of speech.

'But there was a surprise in his will. Dimitri had a sense of humour. He knew how I felt about marriage.'

He answered the look that Kallie hadn't even been aware of giving. His face was carved from stone as he said the words, 'I'll never willingly marry. The woman doesn't exist who I would marry.'

A knife seemed to enter Kallie's heart, stunning her with pain and surprise. She felt herself pulling inwards as if to avoid a blow. Alexandros was oblivious to the havoc he was wreaking within her. The havoc she couldn't even begin to understand. *She* had done this to him?

He cut through her thoughts. 'He made it a condition of his will that I marry within six months of him dying or I won't receive his share of Kouros Shipping.' His mouth twisted. 'It's as if he knew it was the only way I might ever give in to his foolish romantic notions for me.'

Kallie dumbly seized on words to try and avoid feeling the emotions swirling in her head and body.

'But how could you lose everything? Surely his share isn't that big?'

'It's not, but he controlled a key part. As you know, on my father's death, I took full control of the business.'

She felt an unbidden surge of sympathy, remembering the chaos of that time. But Alexandros wouldn't appreciate her concern or interest, certainly not her sympathy. And *how* could she even be feeling sympathetic?

'Dimitri's will states that if I don't marry within the time frame, his share will go to Stakis Shipping.'

Kallie gasped audibly. Stakis Shipping was the mortal enemy. Even she knew that. Underhand deals, rumours of links to drug rings, sex trafficking. They were the black sheep of the shipping world and the only conglomerate powerful enough to possibly take over Kouros Shipping. If what Alexandros said was true, and if he didn't marry, they would be handed an invitation on a silver platter to take a sizeable potshot at his company.

Alexandros couldn't stop the unbidden dart of pleasure seeing the expressions cross her face, at her immediate understanding of the world he came from. He quickly schooled his features again, slightly shocked at how easily the accord had crept in.

'My uncle, in an effort to see me happily wed, has set me up for professional suicide if I don't.'

'I know this is bad but can it really be *that* bad?'

He nodded. 'The share he controlled has strategic importance in the stock markets. It's the link that holds everything else together. *That* gets weakened and it could all crumble. And he knew how abhorrent I find the practices of Constantine Stakis. He's been waiting for an opportunity like this for years. A marriage seems like a small price to pay to keep my family's legacy intact and Stakis out of harm's way.'

That word again. *Marriage.* It crashed into her brain. Kallie shook her head. 'Impossible. I couldn't. I can't.'

Alexandros felt a surge of irritation and anger. Why was he even telling her all this? He slashed a hand through the air.

'This is all beside the point. You don't even deserve an explanation. All you need to know is that I hold the fate of your family in my hands. And the only way you can influence that for the better is by marrying me. If you don't, your family can kiss their fortune goodbye.'

'But that's…ridiculous…archaic. You don't want to tie yourself to me—you hate me.'

He leant forward again. 'Hate is the other side of love, Kallie. I certainly don't hate you.' He swept a look up and down that was so hot she felt it on her skin, 'But I do desire you.'

Little fires of shock raced all over Kallie's body. His eyes had darkened, eyelids lowered slightly so that they looked slumberous.

He desired her?

Why did that make a treacherous curl of excitement lick through her body…and not pain, or disgust?

Her back was so stiff it hurt. Her voice sounded stilted, desperate and glaringly insincere to her ears. 'Well, I certainly don't desire you, Alexandros, so it would be a little one-sided.'

Before she could move out of danger, he had reached across and taken her hand again. Engulfing it with his own. She felt a traitorous pulse start up between her legs and clamped them together. His eyes made a thorough study all the way from her face, the rapid pulse at her neck, down to her chest, where shallow breaths did little to hide her agitation. She could feel her breasts tingle, her nipples hardening, and prayed that he wouldn't see the reaction.

His eyes came back to hers, smug. 'You did once, Kallie, and you still do. If I were to stand up, walk around this table and kiss you right now, you'd be begging for it within seconds.'

The very thought of him doing that made her mouth go dry.

'You flatter yourself…' she said faintly, knowing her words would have no effect. He was coming at her like a two-tonne lorry and there was nothing she could do to stop it. She seized on something, her hand still trapped by his. 'Isabelle Zolanz! You're hardly going to marry me if you're seeing her. Why don't you just marry her? You two are lovers after all…'

Something twisted in her gut when she said that and she had to hide her reaction.

He let her hand go and flicked his dismissively in a very Greek gesture. 'Isabelle is no longer a part of my life.'

Kallie had to suck in a shocked breath at the coldness of his tone. 'It didn't look to me the other night as though she was aware of that.'

'She is now.' His tone brooked no further comment on the subject. Kallie felt a twinge for the other woman and could only imagine how brutal he'd been.

She had to face it. If she hadn't already. The young man she had known, the young man who had once been her friend, her confidant, was gone. In his place was a ruthless man of the world. A truly alpha male. And she had played her part in creating him. She should never have gone to him that night. Regret and recrimination burnt its way through her. But it was too late for all that. Far too late.

She tried to reason with him. 'I won't do it, Alexandros. It's crazy. I'm sorry for what happened. Truly I am. I never meant for anything to happen.'

Liar... You went in search of him that night...

She swallowed and cut off her painful thoughts. 'You can't punish me for something that happened when I was seventeen.'

'Seventeen?' He laughed harshly. 'You were no ingénue, Kallie. I remember the way you were with Giorgio...you had the poor guy panting after you like a dog. You were almost eighteen, about to go to college, on the brink of adulthood—you knew exactly what you were doing.' He waved an impatient hand. 'This isn't about the past any more. In fact, that whole episode just bores me. It's about the present. All the past is doing now is serving to give me a little leverage where you're concerned. A little retribution, sweetened by very strong desire.'

Sadness filled her. He had it all so wrong. Giorgio. She

hadn't thought about him in years. Another friend of her cousins, she'd taken advantage of his dogged pursuit of her to try and make Alexandros jealous. To little effect and much to her shame. But it had been done with the innocence and disregard of a typical teenager. She didn't doubt that Giorgio had been robust enough to accept her rejection and knew he hadn't been too wounded as he had quickly sought the affections of another cousin. Was she to be punished for every little thing?

She shook her head desperately. 'I won't do it. You can't make me.' *Please,* she added silently. He had no idea how much of a punishment this would be.

'Too late. I've made up my mind. If you don't marry me, who would suffer most? I think possibly your uncle Alexei, as he has the most invested. Doesn't he have three grown-up children at college in the States?'

'Stop it…' Fear and panic laced her voice. 'You're a bastard.'

He inclined his head. 'No, Kallie, I'm not.' He lifted a hand and ticked off long fingers. 'I need to get married more or less immediately, you've fallen into my path like a ripe plum, you are available…and you've grown up into a very attractive young woman.'

'So that's it? You only want me now because I come up to your standards of physical perfection?'

He smiled and it didn't reach his eyes. 'You're no image of physical perfection, Kallie, don't flatter yourself, but for some reason I find myself wanting you more than I've wanted any other woman in a long time…so I don't anticipate that there's going to be any hardship on our wedding night when you come to me…'

His insulting choice of words barely impinged her consciousness, she reacted purely to his assertion that she would ever choose willingly to sleep with him. 'I'll never—'

'Yes. You will,' he cut in ruthlessly. 'And I am going to enjoy every moment of this sweet revenge, every step of the way, every piece of flesh that's going to be uncovered as you give yourself to me, as you offer yourself up as you did seven years ago. In the place of the marriage that *you* made sure didn't happen, don't you think when I need a wife now that it's only fair that you step into that role?'

She couldn't control the shiver that shook her frame at his words. And she knew it wasn't a shiver of fear. She *hated* this man. He had her backed into a corner with no way out.

'How can I be sure you'll still deliver on the loan?'

He shrugged. 'I *could* watch your family flounder. Heaven knows, I have the right. But contrary to what you think, Kallie, I'm not that cruel. On our wedding day when I get my convenient wife, you can consider the loan approved.'

She had an overwhelming urge to jump up and run as fast as she could, as far away as she could. But he would find her if she did. She knew that without a doubt. She sank back against the chair, unable to sit up straight in the face of his condemnation.

She looked miserable. 'I don't want them to suffer, despite what you might think.'

And suddenly Kallie had to do something, had to try and make him listen. There had to be a human being in there somewhere. The old Alexandros. She appealed to him now, sitting up straight again.

'Alexandros—'

He started to cut her off and she put up a hand. 'Please. Just let me say something.' Her eyes were an intense green on his. 'I never went to the paper with that story. I would never have done something like that. You *knew* me…' *Better than nearly anyone.*

He said nothing and Kallie searched her brain frantically. 'Why would I have done it, Alexandros? *Why?*'

There was unmistakable tension in his huge frame, just inches away from her. He shrugged dismissively. 'Because you were just one more in a long line of people who thought they could cash in on the Kouros money.' *Except that was a myth by then!*

'Did your father put you up to it, Kallie? See his ticket out of debt? Or did you just do it for the hell of it, to see if you could turn my head yourself? I told you that day I didn't go in for seventeen-year-olds.' His mouth twisted mockingly. 'But if you'd come to me as you are now…'

He flicked an openly appraising look up and down her body. It should have disgusted her. It should have made her angry. But it didn't. It made her feel hot and bothered and confused and out of her depth.

But he wasn't finished. 'To tell the truth, seven years on I'm not much interested in why…' He shook his head. 'You changed, Kallie. The girl I knew would never have tried to seduce me and get someone to photograph the evidence.'

Her insides stung with acute hurt and the humiliation rose up again so sharply she felt sick. To think that he would have believed that of her.

Kallie bit her lip hard and could feel blood. As if his rejection hadn't hurt enough that night, he had to reiterate just how unwelcome her advances had been and how futile it was to try and get him to listen to anything, any explanation.

'I'm sorry. I can't tell you how sorry I am.'

'It's a bit late now.'

His words flayed her like a whip, cutting so deeply that she winced inwardly. 'But really it wasn't like that. I didn't—'

'Give me a break.' Derision and disbelief stamped his features, his mouth a bitter slash. 'There were three people there that night, you, me and whoever your loyal photographer was. Pity they were so amateur…but they got enough.'

She slumped back again, defeated and diminished by his derision and cruelty. And now that she knew what he wanted, all avenues of escape were closed off. She couldn't assert her innocence any further, and she couldn't explain what had happened as that would involve someone who wouldn't be able to handle this much more dangerous Alexandros. Eleni had come up to Kallie at her parents' funeral, nearly hysterical with remorse and guilt. She'd told her everything—how she'd followed Kallie out to the patio, taken the picture, hacked into her e-mail and sent in the story.

For one blissful moment, unaware of *him* across the table, Kallie's mind was fixed on that awful day of such tragedy. The added pain when Eleni had revealed the truth. Kallie had always had her suspicions but, still, to hear it explained... She'd been shocked and angry. Dismayed, hurt. About to lash back, already filled with grief and now anger. But Eleni's husband had stepped in. He'd explained everything, exactly why Eleni had been acting so on the edge. Which was the reason why Kallie couldn't defend herself now.

She'd discovered that her cousin had had a nervous breakdown, and had been undergoing intense therapy after suffering numerous miscarriages. Kallie had seen the pain on Eleni's husband's face. Her fight had left her. It had only been after that incident and with the benefit of maturity and hindsight that Kallie could see just how Eleni had also been captivated by him. And how highly strung and manipulative her cousin had always been. Especially with regard to Alexandros.

The man who sat opposite her now, looking so calm and so devastatingly at ease as he toyed with her life. He had been on a mission ever since he'd seen her again. It was as if she'd awakened the sleeping dragon. And she had to take it, had no choice.

She didn't need to remind herself that, despite Eleni's involvement, if *she* hadn't pursued Alexandros that night, there wouldn't have been an excuse for a story in the first place. She had no one to blame for this except herself. No matter what the consequences had been, or how unwittingly she'd played a part. And now he held the future of Demarchis Shipping in his hands.

She lifted dull eyes that were mute with an appeal she was unaware of. Weary beyond belief.

'I have no choice, do I?'

He answered slowly, 'Of course you do, Kallie, we always have a choice. Yours is very simple. If you walk away now, your uncle will not receive one euro from me, and as he's been turned down by every bank, and no other shipping company will touch him, he and, consequently, the family, will be ruined. If you agree to marry me, he'll be fine.'

Some choice…

She asked the fateful question. 'How long would we…?'

He shrugged one broad shoulder. 'For as long as I want, Kallie. The day you start to bore me, the day I lose interest, is the day we'll divorce and you can consider this marriage over.'

CHAPTER FIVE

AND just like that, from the moment she'd fatefully bumped into Alexandros Kouros again, he'd come back into her life with the force of an atom bomb and turned everything upside down and inside out. And all because he needed a convenient wife. Someone who wouldn't expect a happy ever after when he discarded them by the wayside of his fast-paced life that had no room for a real marriage.

Kallie moved through the next three weeks as though in some kind of a fog. Where once Alexandros had been blissfully absent, now he was everywhere she turned. In her office, at the door of her flat, on the phone, barking terse instructions. The paparazzi had snapped them coming out of the Hotel de Crillon that night after dinner. Kallie had been so shell-shocked coming out that she'd barely noticed the flashing, popping bulbs. And only the next day when she'd opened the papers had she seen the pictures. Headlines screamed of a possible romance…which was promptly confirmed by Alexandros's PR people. Before she even had time to draw breath, the net was being drawn tighter and tighter around her. And no doubt, she thought bitterly, he saw the justice in dragging her name through the papers now, too.

She drew the line, however, when he sent over a credit card one day close to the wedding with an order to kit herself out, and called him angrily on the phone.

'I will *not* be paraded like some gilded lily. And I will *not* go and buy clothes with your money, to your specifications. You may be as good as blackmailing me to buy yourself a convenient wife but I will not be your chattel, Alexandros. I've been dressing myself successfully with no complaints for some time now and I intend to keep doing so.'

'Well, believe me, you're going to need a little gilding to be my wife. Your look is far too casually natural—'

Kallie gasped in consternation, seething. 'Weren't you the one who implied that I might have had work done? Make up your mind!'

He was quite unconcerned, drawling, 'That was before I saw you again properly. I'm quite sure now that you've had no…surgical enhancements and, believe me, I'm looking forward to finding out for sure.'

That was when Kallie slammed the phone down. She cut up the credit card and sent it back to Alexandros with a courier. Which he received with a wry smile. The first woman, *ever,* to refuse his money. He wondered what game Kallie might be playing but couldn't deny that he was growing more and more intrigued by the day. Having to take a convenient wife was turning out to be far more entertaining than he'd first anticipated.

The day before the civil marriage was to take place at the office of the *mairie* on the Place Du Panthéon, Kallie was meeting her uncle for lunch near his office on the Champs Elysées. The Arc de Triomphe was a mere shape in the distance as she steeled herself and went into the restaurant.

He stood as she approached and they kissed on both cheeks in a warm greeting. She hadn't seen him since that night at the Ritz. They'd spoken on the phone when she'd delivered her news of the wedding and now she couldn't put off the inevitable any more. Finally, after she'd prevaricated for as long as possible, he got to the point. Taking her hand across the table, he said gently, 'Kallie, darling, you know how important to me you are, you're like another daughter.'

'I know…' She tried to keep the emotion out of her voice, aching to be able to confide in someone, anyone.

'Are you telling me the truth about Alexandros?' He shook his head. 'I just find it a little hard to believe that you bumped into him that night and have had this whirlwind romance. I know him, Kallie. He's not given to random romantic whims…and *this*, well, it's completely out of character. Especially with the history between you. I remember how angry he was. That story in the paper—'

Kallie cut him off before he could delve too deeply into the past—the present was hard enough to deal with. 'Alexei. Please. believe me when I say you don't have to worry about anything.' She crossed her fingers under the table on a superstitious reflex. 'It is true. We met that night and… I don't know.' She shrugged and pasted a bland smile on her face. 'He's changed. Seven years is a long time. He doesn't harbour any grudges.' Her fingers were clenched so tightly that Kallie could feel the blood flow stopping. 'Trust me, Alexei, I don't want you to think about it, really. I *want* to marry Alexandros.'

She prayed that her hopelessly romantic uncle wouldn't push her to say anything about love. He looked unconvinced for a long moment but then something seemed to pass over his face and he smiled. 'I do trust you, Kallie.' He squeezed her hand. 'I know it can happen like that. After all, didn't I fall in love with your Aunt Petra in just a week?'

Kallie smiled weakly.

A rogue part of her needed to check something. 'Alexei, that night at the Ritz, you mentioned that you'd had to go to Alexandros. Is there anything you want to tell me?'

He paled and Kallie's heart fell. Confirmation…as if she needed it at this stage. Even so, a tiny part of her had clung to some mad, irrational hope. He blustered slightly, clearly embarrassed, his macho Greek pride painfully evident and obviously the reason why he hadn't said anything about the loan. 'My dear, don't be ridiculous, we're just doing business, that's all.'

She read far more into his reactions than he suspected. She'd checked up on what Alexandros had said and every word he'd uttered had been true. Things were even worse than she'd anticipated. She didn't know how Alexei had been managing for so long without a loan. His efforts to secure loans elsewhere were dismayingly documented in financial papers. Guilt made her feel cold inside again. If she'd been the slightest bit interested, she would have noticed. Her shares had long been sucked into the haemorrhaging business.

She had to comfort herself that at least this way she was keeping Alexandros's lust for revenge to herself. No one else would ever know and the Demarchis shipping fleet would be safe. It was cold comfort, however, as she said goodbye to her still uncomfortable-looking uncle. She'd never felt so alone and vulnerable in her life. As she walked back down one of the most famous boulevards in the world, she felt as if everything was closing in on her and her last chance of possibly avoiding her fate had just disappeared. Snuffed out like the light of a candle. She shivered in the warm spring air.

When she got back to her office Alexandros was waiting for her. Her whole body stiffened in blatant rejection of what was to come the next day. He noted it with narrowed eyes as he watched her walk in from behind her desk. As at home as if he sat there every day. He made a thorough study of her, up and down, taking in the black pencil skirt, the cream high-necked shirt, which she was supremely grateful for now.

'Can I help you with something?'

He uncurled his tall length from the chair and came around the desk. Devastatingly compelling in a dark suit and dark shirt. Kallie took a step back. The room seemed to have become as hot as hell in seconds. Alexandros flicked his head to indicate the window and looked out. Kallie walked over very warily, keeping a good distance, but even that couldn't stop the frisson of awareness running through her.

Outside, swarming on the pavement, were what seemed to be hundreds of photographers. The circus that surrounded Alexandros Kouros. She hadn't seen them before as she'd come in through another entrance. He came and stood beside her. Her skin prickled uncomfortably. So far he hadn't said a word. The moment seemed to stretch for ever. And finally with silky deadliness he said softly, 'You see that? They're all going to be waiting outside the office of the *mairie* tomorrow. Waiting to see you arrive, go in and then come out on my arm. And they're going to get the pictures they want. If you're planning any little surprises, like not turning up, then I will find you, Kallie, and I will take you as far away from here as I can, and we will be married where you will have no escape.'

She turned to face him, dread in her body at his cold tone. This stranger before her. Bitterness laced her voice. 'I've already told you I'd marry you. I'd do anything to save my family from ruin. Even if it means marrying you and subjecting myself to a period of purgatory.'

He turned to face her, his face stamped with arrogance and a sensuality that even now called to her on some base, carnal level. She hated him. She knew she kept telling herself that…and knew it felt as though she was trying to convince herself.

He reached out a finger and trailed it along her jaw. She clenched it and he tapped where it bulged out against her smooth skin.

'Such dramatic language, Kallie. When you set me up all those years ago, when *I* was considered as close as family, it made me very wary. I'm just warning you what will happen if you decide to leave your family to their fate. That's all.'

He was so far off base from how Kallie felt that her head

swam. She would never, *ever* do something to hurt her family. It seemed as if everything, every conversation that had ever passed between them, had turned to poisoned ashes. And amounted to nothing. He'd decided to judge her solely based on what he'd perceived her to have done seven years ago.

She straightened her shoulders and stuck her chin out.

'I will be there tomorrow, Alexandros, and, believe me, you're going to be sorry you ever married me.'

'Somehow I don't think so. But I admire your attempt at bravado. One other thing. I've asked members of our families, just as a little added...insurance.'

Kallie felt her throat clog and wanted nothing more than to hit him right in the solar plexus, wipe that smug smirk from his face. But then he snaked a hand around the back of her head through her hair and pulled her softly to him. Panic coursed through her. Her hands came up in an instinctive and classic defense pose between them.

'What do you think you're doing?' She tingled with anticipation.

'Just the one other thing I need to confirm for myself before I make you my wife...check the levels of compatibility...'

'Levels of—'

And before she could speak another word, his head had dipped, daylight disappeared and his mouth was on hers. Warm and intoxicating and hot and...words disappeared. Kallie found her hands resting against his broad chest, his heat coursing over her skin, making *her* heat up all over. She felt herself wanting to melt into him, against his hard length. His lips moved against hers, hard and insistent. A completely instinctive unbidden response made her open her mouth and at the first touch of his tongue to hers, an explosive heat erupted deep in her belly.

She felt him pulling her in tighter, lifting her up against him. She wanted nothing more than to give in...lean against him, savour the support. Her eyes flew open. His were shut. Hidden.

What was wrong with her? What was she thinking?

She welcomed reality, letting it flow through her like ice, dousing the flame of desire that wanted to burst into flame like a flash fire. His mouth was still moving over hers, and a weak part of her was an insistent voice saying, G*ive in, give in.*

She clenched her hands into fists with a huge effort and pushed against his chest. It was like a steel wall, immovable. She twisted her mouth away from his and was shocked at how ragged her breathing was. Pushing her chest against his, making her very aware of how her breasts had begun to ache, her nipples so hard they chafed against her bra. He tried to twist her head back and Kallie struggled in earnest now, beating against his chest, her breath coming more and more ragged and jerky. She still couldn't speak.

He finally loosened his hold and Kallie used it to push herself out of his arms, staggering back against the desk behind her. If it hadn't been there, she would have fallen to the floor, she knew that for sure. Her hands clung to the ridges behind her, her entire body pulsed, heat melted the ice and she had the strongest urge to throw herself back into his arms and beg him to kiss her again. She tried to bring her breathing under control and marvelled that kissing him so chastely at seventeen certainly hadn't prepared her for *this...*

She was undone. In the space of seconds. Had given in spectacularly before she'd stopped, letting him know of her weak acquiescence. She couldn't look up and saw his feet come into her line of vision on the floor in front of her. A hand came under her chin, tipping it up to face him, and she shut her eyes.

'Kallie, closing your eyes isn't going to make the truth go away.'

Against her better judgment she opened them and tensed herself for his look of triumph. But it wasn't there. Instead was a look she couldn't read and his eyes were dark, darker than she'd ever seen them. With deep glowing embers in their depths. Embers that *she* had lit? The thought made something rip through her. She trembled.

She had to try and claw back some modicum of dignity and found a voice from somewhere.

'Truth…' She didn't even have the energy to voice it as a question.

'That there's enough electricity between us to power the national grid.' His eyes fell to her mouth and Kallie felt it quiver in response as if it were begging for his own lips again. 'And that tomorrow we get married and…*this* we'll come back to. We'll have plenty of time on our honeymoon.'

Kallie opened her mouth and couldn't speak for a few seconds. *Honeymoon!* 'That's ridiculous. There's no way this is going to happen.' Panic was making her sound breathless. 'I am not going anywhere with you for any honeymoon. I have to work, I can't just leave—'

He put a finger to her mouth. 'Oh, yes, you are. It's part of the deal. Make sure you're packed…'

Alexandros strode through the mass of photographers outside Kallie's office. Unlike with other celebrities, who they would crush around, intimidate into submission, a space was left around Alexandros. That held a certain kind of respect. As if they knew that with one swipe of his hand, one word, he could do some serious damage. He ignored the barrage of questions and got into the back of his car. The blacked-out windows concealed him from view immediately.

He tersely instructed his driver to take the long way back to his office. He needed to think, to collect himself. And this was as alien a concept to him as the thought of taking public transport. But the fact of the matter was that his body still throbbed with a level of arousal he'd never experienced before.

What the hell had just happened back there?

He ran a hand through his hair and stared unseeingly out

of the window. He hadn't planned on kissing Kallie. But when she'd walked in, so prim and proper in her buttoned-up shirt and tight skirt that drew the eye to the toned length of thigh, he hadn't been able to resist.

All he did know was the moment he'd taken Kallie into his arms he hadn't felt like he'd thought he would. Oh, he'd felt the desire. That had been like a neon sign that lit up whenever he was near her...it hadn't been that. It had been something else, something he'd never felt before. He'd expected to feel detached...but he hadn't. He'd felt anticipation that had gone beyond the mere physical. As if he'd finally had something within his grasp that he'd been searching for. A sigh had gone through him when his mouth had touched hers. *A sigh of relief...*

His whole body tensed in the back of the car in absolute rejection of his thoughts. And for the first time since seeing Kallie again, he questioned whether or not he was doing the right thing. His mouth pulled into a thin line. The fact of the matter was, though, that he'd left it too late now. He would need to find a wife to marry within twenty-four hours if he was to make the deadline of Dimitri's will. And he certainly couldn't afford to let this slip through his hands merely because he was having these...doubts.

For Alexandros, who never ever doubted a decision he'd made, this was also a new concept. Not a welcome one. His mind even seized on Isabelle for a moment. He grimaced. There were plenty of women who would be only too happy to comply with his need for an immediate wife. But he had Kallie so well trussed now, not to mention the arousal that hummed in his every vein, why shouldn't he use her? Have her. Sate himself with her.

After all, wasn't this just meant to be just a diversion for him? An amusement? A timely revenge and a way to get his needs met, both in and out of bed?

It was only then that the belated thought struck him—he'd called at her office to see if she'd received the pre-nuptial agreement. He'd never before had a lapse like that in his concentration. He found himself ignoring the need to dwell on why he'd been acting so out of character and quickly instructed his bodyguard to go back and pick it up.

It was a couple of minutes after Alexandros had left that Kallie fully realised that he'd gone. She still hadn't moved. She felt as though she'd been flung into another dimension. He'd just kissed her, she told herself rationally. *And told you that he expects you to go on a honeymoon…*

She felt dizzy, disjointed…her head was fuzzy. She went on shaky legs and sat down behind her desk. Her glazed eyes took in a note on the top of her pad. The big brusque handwriting that could only belong to one person. *Him.*

'Please sign the pre-nuptial agreement and send it back.'

Kallie read it and reread it, finally, slowly coming back to her senses. She heard the bells of a church ring ominously in the distance. Like a nail going into a coffin, her fate was sealed, this was it. He hadn't even had the decency to tell her this much. He'd gone from issuing terse instructions to leaving curt notes. He'd waltzed into her office, tested her out like some Arabian prince buying a new girl for his harem. To see if she met with his approval. Her mouth twisted, she couldn't help the shudder of reaction that went through her. Well, apparently she did. Lucky her.

Her assistant popped her head around the door at that moment, diverting her thoughts, and when Kallie nodded she came in. Holding out a manila envelope, she said, 'Sorry, this came earlier, but I got distracted when Alexandros…' She blushed prettily and Kallie scowled. 'Sorry. When Mr Kouros arrived.'

She beat a hasty retreat and Kallie scowled even harder. Another female ready to drop at his feet. Was no one immune to the man's charm? She ripped the envelope open and a sheaf of papers fell out. The agreement. Kallie skimmed it feeling numb. It outlined the terms of the marriage—basically she was entitled to nothing in the event of the divorce. That didn't surprise her. It also specified the terms of the loan to her uncle, the generosity of which surprised her. He genuinely was reserving all punishment just for her. It suited her fine. She didn't want to touch a penny of his money.

She signed quickly, without thinking, and shoved the papers back into the envelope. About to call Cécile back in, she looked up when a shape appeared at the doorway. She almost thought it was him until she saw his bodyguard come in. She pulled herself together and held out the envelope.

'Mr Kouros sent you for this?'

He took it and left.

The reality was stark. From now on, as long as he desired, for as long as they would have the reaction they'd both just had to a simple kiss, she was Alexandros Kouros's property. For better or worse.

CHAPTER SIX

'For better or worse…'

The words swam over Kallie's head. She stood in the *mairie*'s office with Alexandros by her side. Everything seemed to be swimming, ever since she'd come in the door with Alexei and seen Alexandros standing there. In a steel-grey suit, looking so tall and dark and vibrantly handsome that she'd stumbled on her walk towards him.

Members of both their families were seated behind them. The speed with which the last few weeks had flown, the reaction of her body just standing beside this man…was overwhelming. She struggled to fix her gaze on a point in the distance and only belatedly realised that Alexandros was turning her towards him, having been told he could kiss his wife.

His wife…

Kallie looked up into his face, helpless now. Bound to him in front of everyone, in front of society. Wordlessly she tried to communicate with him. Willing the harsh, stark lines of his face to relax…just for a moment so that she could reach something of the person she'd once known. But they didn't. That person was gone. As his head bent towards hers for the second time in two days, she felt every treacherous cell in her body leaping in response, hungering for his touch, his mouth on hers. She fought it, though…tensed her entire body and willed herself with every fibre of her being not to have the same reaction as yesterday.

He took her face in his hands, tilting it up to his. Why did he have to do that? Why couldn't he just plant a dry kiss on her lips, quick and efficient? With his big hands cupping her jaw, face close to hers, his thumbs feathering across her cheeks, she felt her body temperature soar and imagined he must be able to feel her heart about to explode from her chest.

Slowly, and surrounded by a hushed quiet in the room, his head came closer and closer. Kallie's eyes were trapped by his. When the drowning sensation became too much she closed them, the lids feeling heavy. And then...his mouth angled over hers and fitted so perfectly that her every nerve ending seemed to meet and connect with every one of his. The reaction in her blood to just the touch of his lips to hers made her knees weak and she had to put out her hands and cling to his waist in an effort to stay upright. The scent of him intoxicated her, his body heat enveloped her in a haze of sensual warmth. Just like yesterday—and she was being played like a violin, *again*.

He had intended for it to be a quick kiss. As much as he wanted Kallie with a desire that was fast running out of control, Alexandros had no intention of being surrounded by people when he plumbed the depths of that lush mouth again. So this was just going to be chaste, dry—certainly not *this*. This *fire* that had taken over his blood as soon as he'd touched her skin, as soon as their lips had made contact. Light exploded behind his eyes. And when he felt her eyelashes flutter against his cheeks, it tugged at a thread of a memory from long ago...

When he felt the tremor run through her, felt her hands reach out to steady herself, it was too much. He was only human. He pulled her in close and dropped a hand to her back to anchor her against his body. The crowd, witnesses forgotten. The world was reduced to this moment, this woman, these lips under his which were opening to him so enticingly, with such potent sweetness. And he was lost in a maelstrom of passion that made him shake with the effort not to stroke and explore and plunder the moist, hot interior.

A child's cry pierced Alexandros's consciousness and went through him like shock of cold water. Feeling every impulse in his body wanting to stay, he somehow managed to pull back. When he opened his eyes they felt dazed, hazy, and Kallie's were still shut, her lips pink and plump, lashes curled against her cheeks. He could feel the uneven raggedness of her breath.

Kallie knew he had stopped kissing her. She knew it like a bizarre intellectual fact but could not seem to open her eyes or move. When she felt him tap a finger against her cheek it unlocked the stasis she'd been stuck in. Her eyes flew open to meet his. They were full of heat and darkness. A sound made her look and when she turned her head she saw their relations staring, open-mouthed. She felt her insides go cold, even as she felt hectic colour flood her cheeks.

Kallie couldn't look at him. Instead, she smiled brightly, breaking the spell that seemed to encompass the room. The crowd started clapping and Alexandros took her hand and led the way back outside. Only when Kallie was sure she had regained some semblance of control did she turn to him. Before they were sucked into a round of congratulatory hugs, she said coolly, 'Don't think that just because I can put on a performance for the family, it'll be the same in private.'

His face visibly darkened and Kallie rejoiced in needling him, even a little, even as she had to realise that this was not a man to trifle with. He would exact revenge for every petty point she scored. She was saved from a caustic response as they were surrounded in seconds and before she knew it they were getting out of a car and stepping into an exclusive discreet hotel for the lunch reception.

A few hours later, the only thing keeping Kallie back from the brink of sheer white-knuckled panic was the sight laid out in front of her in the glittering ballroom. Members of her family that she hadn't seen in years and some of Alexandros's family were seated at little round tables dotted around the room. Petra caught her eye beside her beloved husband Alexei, and waved at Kallie, who waved weakly back.

When they'd come out of the office earlier, into the Place Du Panthéon with its massive monument to the glory of secularism dominating the magnificent square, her uncle's wife had rushed up to Kallie with tears in her eyes and, taking advantage of Alexandros talking to someone else, had whispered in her ear, 'Kallie, darling, I'm so happy for you. When Alexei told me about how you two got together, I have to say I was a little worried, but after seeing you now…' She'd raised her hands high. 'It's obvious you're in love.'

Kallie couldn't believe that people patently saw what they wanted to see. Not what was right under their noses. She was doing this against her will and no one could see it.

The lunch was finally over and Kallie could absent herself from Alexandros's disturbing presence beside her. Thankfully he'd agreed that they wouldn't make speeches—that would have been pushing things too far, even for Kallie. She excused herself to go to the bathroom and once inside splashed water on her wrists and on her neck to cool her pulse which had been racing since that kiss.

She sent up silent thanks that he obviously hadn't thought to invite Eleni and her husband, and then chastised herself for her churlish thought. Perhaps Eleni was back in hospital again? She looked at her pained face in the mirror. Why couldn't she be more like him? Emotionally cut off from the neck down?

Wearily she straightened her hair, fixed her make-up and made her way back into the huge room, firmly diverting any line of thinking that involved the future or even later that evening. She hadn't yet figured out how to handle Alexandros because there was one thing she was certain of—she was not going to be sleeping with him.

Alexandros couldn't focus on the conversation around him. Kallie's shining head stood out like a glowing beacon from all the darker ones. He watched her progress as she walked back into the room, the only member of the family who wasn't entirely Greek on both sides. She'd tied her hair back in a loose, tumbled knot. With an orchid caught in the glossy strands and minimal make-up, Alexandros thought he'd never seen anyone lovelier.

Her outfit was simple, highlighting her natural elegance, and he had to admit that he hadn't been entirely fair when he'd criticised the way she dressed. A knee-length cream silk dress with a gossamer-light golden-coloured shawl, high strappy golden sandals that drew the eye to slim ankles and shapely calves. And when she moved, like now, to greet one of her family, the silk of the dress moved with her and tightened across her hips… again, he was blown away by the beauty that had been lying in wait through her younger years. Yet hadn't she always possessed it? Her eyes had always been that distinctive blue-green colour, her lips always as soft… Desire surged through him fast and urgent as he thought of the kiss in the registry office.

Acting on blind impulse, he strode through the crowd. It was time to get out of there and take her with him.

Kallie was still talking to one of her aunts when she felt a presence behind her like an electric frisson, and her skin tingled in reaction. She closed her eyes briefly in despair and when she opened them again a strong arm had come around her waist. She didn't look up at Alexandros but smiled brightly at the older woman and chattered on nonsensically. She could feel the tension in the man beside her as his arm tightened on her waist, causing a whirlpool of sensations in her belly.

'Are you ready to go?'

As if she had a choice, Kallie thought slightly hysterically. She just nodded, realising that she actually did want to get away from the attention, the looks, the questions. They said their goodbyes.

In the lobby, with her hand in the firm grip of his, Kallie stumbled, trying to keep up with his long-legged stride. And in that moment, the enormity of what had just happened hit her. They were about to walk outside, away from any last piece of protection. She would be alone with Alexandros and he would expect

She stopped dead in her tracks, forcing him to come to a halt, too. He looked back, a dark look on his face. 'What is it?'

'What is it? *What is it?*' Kallie's voice was rising as her fear rose, too, like an unstoppable volcano that had just blown its top. She yanked her hand out of Alexandros's with an effort and stood there shaking.

'What is wrong with you? This isn't real...this is a farce. And everyone in there thinks that we're in love, that this is a proper marriage.' She started to back away, back towards the room, babbling, 'I can't do it. I can't do this. I'm going to tell them. I'll work for Alexei, I'll do anything to help him get another loan... But don't make me... I just can't do this, I can't—'

With lightning speed Alexandros reached her as she turned and hauled her into his arms, his mouth crashing down on hers, silencing her words. She struggled and fought but he kept kissing her, and kissing her. Finally he felt her body grow pliant, and her mouth had softened. He'd forgotten the reason he'd started to kiss her in the first place.

Kallie forgot, too, in a shamingly short amount of time. The anger drained away under the intense building of desire that started low down and rose throughout her entire body. Her hands were trapped against Alexandros's chest and she revelled in the close contact with the hard muscle under his shirt. When she felt the strength of his arousal through the flimsy silk of her dress she couldn't pull away. Her hips rocked, aching to be closer, and he pulled her up and into the cradle of his lap.

When he lifted his head after long minutes. Kallie's mouth clung...until the cool air swept over her skin as someone came out of the door behind them. She tensed immediately and her eyes flew open, clashing with dark brown ones. This time there was a look of triumph on his face.

She was still too stunned by the strength of her reaction to do anything, feel anything other than the blood that coursed through her with the force of a crashing wave.

He smiled down at her, and trailed a finger along her jaw. He, unlike her, seemed to be capable of speaking, of being rational.

'It's too late, Kallie. We're married. As you seem to have conveniently forgotten, you've already signed the agreement that seals my promise of the loan, and this...' He moved his hips slightly, his erection sliding tantalisingly against the silk-covered apex of her thighs. The burning desire still held her in its grip. '*This* is very much the next part of the plan.'

She was held and mesmerised by his eyes. She had to wonder for the first moment since seeing him again what he would do when he discovered she was woefully inexperienced. That suddenly made her brain freeze. He wouldn't want to sleep with a novice. She wasn't a virgin but may as well be compared to him! She should tell him now before they went any further. This was the thing that would make him dump her faster than a hot piece of coal. She opened her mouth to speak but nothing came out. Two sides of her went to war, the side that wanted very badly to get away right now, forget she'd ever seen Alexandros again, and the other side that wanted nothing more than for him to lay her down, right where they were, and take her to paradise and back.

They were still locked together, as close as they could be. She had to say something, she couldn't be this weak. A flashing pop made Kallie flinch in his arms as suddenly, within what seemed like seconds, they were surrounded by paparazzi. The hotel doormen, along with bodyguards that had materialised out of thin air, were trying to beat them back, and in the mayhem that followed Kallie was bundled out and into a car with Alexandros so fast that they were speeding away before she could even get her breath, never mind launch into a declaration of her sexual inexperience.

CHAPTER SEVEN

When she was finally able to articulate a word she bit out, 'Are you going to tell me where we're going?'

The thought of a honeymoon, just her and Alexandros together, was causing waves of panic through Kallie's tense body.

Alexandros looked at her. Her arms were folded across her chest. Everything about her screamed, *Get out!* And made him more determined than ever to slake his lust, experience the passion that ignited with just a touch of their mouths.

He forced himself to relax, to try and dampen the spark that was ready to be fanned into a burning flame at the slightest provocation...or encouragement, which he figured was unlikely in the near future.

'Our bags are following so we're going straight to the airport.'

Was he being deliberately obtuse? Kallie emitted a frustrated sigh.

'And is this a magic mystery tour or are you going to tell me where we're going?'

She was all too aware of the strained edge in her voice. Alexandros regarded her coolly from his seat. Looking casual and relaxed and at ease, when she felt as tightly wound as a spring.

'We're going to my villa just outside Athens.'

Kallie frowned and automatically slipped into the familiar Greek name for her grandmother. 'The villa beside *ya ya*'s?'

He nodded. 'My mother has moved into town. It's easier for her, and closer to the doctors if she needs them. I've had it completely refurbished in the interim.'

She'd bet he had. And she could only imagine the opulence. It had always been very grand, effortlessly overshadowing her grandparents' more humble villa, with its deceptively simple design.

She saw that they were driving into a small airfield, approaching a private jet. She tried to quell her panic and looked at Alexandros as if to block out the evidence that very shortly they would be on a plane, flying to Athens, to be alone. She knew she was talking quickly, inanely.

'I haven't been back there since *ya ya* died. Her house is sitting empty now. Some of the family go there sometimes, I think, but…'

A sudden upsurge of sadness gripped Kallie, taking her by surprise. That house held such special memories for her and the thought of seeing it again without her beloved grandmother hit home.

She didn't see how Alexandros's gaze narrowed on her face. 'Is this your first visit back to Athens since then?'

And was that moisture in her eyes?

She swallowed the lump in her throat and looked at him, shaking her head, desperately willing the emotion down. 'Not to Athens, just to her house…'

She'd had no idea the thought of going back there would affect her so strongly.

The car came to a smooth halt and thankfully she clambered out into the cool air. Anything to avoid that intense, laser-like gaze. Within minutes they were ensconced in plush cream leather seats in the plane, sitting opposite one another. Kallie felt a little more under control again. She couldn't be her normal self around Alexandros. But it was so hard, watching everything she said, having to control every impulse. She was used to living honestly, openly. But, of course, they were the last things he believed her to be. Open and honest. As they took off and she avoided meeting the dark gaze she could feel resting on her, Kallie had to admit to herself that being open and honest hadn't exactly worked for her in the past. She'd found out that people didn't appreciate it. Would step all over it...

A host of conflicting uncomfortable emotions were ripping through Alexandros. He took in Kallie's averted profile, the way she swallowed convulsively. He'd seen the sheen of tears in her eyes in the car and it had thrown him completely. He'd even found himself about to ask if she'd prefer to stay at his apartment in Athens, rather than go to the villa. His jaw clenched. Thank goodness he'd come to his senses. Kallie Demarchis at the age of seventeen had shown a mercenary streak that had stunned him. Seven years on, it would only have been honed and developed.

The only reason she'd be letting tears fall would be to manipulate a situation for her own ends. And he had to concede that she must be seething...perhaps even plotting something. How could she not? He'd made sure that she would get nothing from the marriage and he'd checked up on her financial status. The money she would have got from her shares, which would have gone into six figures, was long gone. The girl had expensive tastes. Goodness only knew what she had spent the money on.

He looked away moodily and stared out the window at the ground dropping away beneath them. Bed her and get her out of his system. That's all he wanted to do. He didn't have to think about anything else. He sent up a fervent prayer that by the end of the two weeks he'd be thoroughly sated and he could file for divorce. He'd even told his solicitor to have the divorce papers drawn up and ready, not intending this to be a long marriage *at all*.

Kallie sent a quick curious look to Alexandros and was shocked to see his face in such stern lines. She'd felt his withdrawal, as if he was pulling in, pulling away from her. And as if to confirm her suspicions, he looked at her then, but it was so cold, so black that she had to repress a shiver.

'Are you hungry?' he surprised her by asking brusquely,

Kallie shook her head and felt a wave of tiredness wash over her, which she succumbed to with relief and not a little cowardice. She was confused by her own turbulent desires. She welcomed some respite, however flimsy. Allowing her eyes to close, shutting out the evocative and disturbing image of Alexandros, her body sank into the reclining seat.

Kallie woke to a gentle touch and found the stewardess standing over her. Someone had put a blanket over her, too.

'Mrs Kouros, we're landing in a few minutes.'

For a second she was about to assert that she wasn't Mrs Kouros until she remembered that she was. She scrambled up inelegantly, relieved to see that Alexandros was missing from his seat. She pushed her hands through her tumbled hair and secured it back again. The orchid came out in her hand and she looked at it. What had possessed her to put it in her hair earlier? She threw it down on the table beside her, disgusted with herself that she might have somehow unconsciously done it for *him*. She wanted to get out of the dress, which clung far too much, and get into jeans…or overalls, or something. Anything else.

And who had put the blanket over her? The thought that it might have been him made her insides liquefy. Silly, she chided herself. It was far more likely to have been the stewardess. She looked up and saw Alexandros emerge from a cabin at the back. He looked pristine. Her cheeks felt hot and her eyes sticky from sleep as he came towards her.

'Good, you're awake. We're landing now.'

She just nodded, didn't trust herself to speak, and diverted her attention to the view outside. The vista of Athens in the distance got closer and closer until they finally landed. A warm feeling spread through her as she saw the familiar skyline. Coming back to Athens had always felt like coming home, and she'd missed it.

Once they had landed everything happened so quickly it was a blur. They were out of the plane and ensconced in a luxury four-wheel-drive with tinted windows within minutes. One bodyguard in the front with the driver, the other following in another vehicle with the luggage. She was caught out by feeling suddenly happy at the thought of being back here. She needed to feel close to the Greek earth again.

The warm air caressed Kallie's skin like silk as she stepped from the vehicle outside the Kouros villa. Dusk was claiming the sky, lines of pink strewn across it like ribbons as the sun fell. Her own family villa was hidden in the trees just a couple of hundred yards away. She sucked in the warm spring air and drank in the sight of Alexandros's home. It had always had a slightly crumbling grandeur that Kallie had been in awe of, but the refurbishment was total and stunning. It was painted a warm off-white that reflected the glow of the setting sun. Its low front and flat roof made it look almost unassuming, but the wide veranda leading up to the huge front door hinted at the luxury that lay inside.

What kept the villa from looking almost too linear, flat, were the trees that lined the entire front façade. Tall and willowy, the typical pine trees of the region were spaced in such a way as to enhance the view of the villa, not detract from it. Kallie knew the first modest impression was deceptive.

The villa was built into the hillside, almost wrapped around it, in fact, giving it two stunning views over Athens—one from the garden, the other from the pool that was at the bottom of several levels cut into the earth, among trees and olive groves.

Just then the front door opened and a familiar full-bodied figure rushed out and down the steps, a round brown face wreathed in smiles. Kallie tried to keep track of the rapid Greek as Alexandros's long-time housekeeper greeted him with a big hug. But when it came to Kallie Thea merely skated a glance over her and barely acknowledged her. Kallie's stomach dropped. So Thea hadn't forgiven her either. There had been a time when she had been the housekeeper's favourite, when she used to sneak over and spend happy hours in the kitchen learning how to make traditional Greek recipes. But Thea had never forgiven Kallie for the way Alexandros had been treated. Kallie had tried to explain, feeling that out of everyone Thea might listen to her, but to no avail. And with seven years gone by, Kallie knew she'd be even less likely to listen now.

In the entrance hall Thea called a young maid and asked her to show Kallie up to her room, as coolly as if she'd never even known her. Kallie was determined not to reveal how hurt she was and followed the young girl upstairs. She was relieved to see that it wasn't the master bedroom, although her relief fled when Alexandros appeared at the door, leaning against it nonchalantly.

He took her in, standing like a startled fawn caught in the headlights. The raw, visceral way he felt, the almost overwhelming urge he had to go over and tip her onto the bed, made him very, very wary. The maid had mistakenly brought her to a guest room. He'd intended her to be in *his* room with *him*…but now he wasn't so sure that was the best idea, despite the clamour of his pulse. He was a civilised man of the world. Not someone ruled by his primitive desires, like some kind of caveman. He made a decision to play around with the truth slightly.

'I've given you your own room, Kallie,' he said as he came

in. She backed away against the far wall, watching with huge eyes as he walked to another door and opened it. *That* led into the master bedroom. He left it open.

'There's no lock in this door… Like I said in Paris, you'll come to me. And I'll be ready when you do.'

He walked over and stood very close. He reached out a hand and trailed fingers over her collar-bone, which was bared in the dress. Her breath hitched. The energy crackled between them, like a live wire as his hand went down, lower and lower until his fingers grazed the slopes of her breast. Watching her intently, Alexandros let his hand cup one breast. Her nipple sprang to immediate hardness against the silk of her dress and pushed insistently against his palm. He struggled not to haul her close and take her mouth with his, ravaging her breast with his hand.

Kallie's breath had long stopped and she'd given up trying to figure out how she still stood. She could feel a bead of sweat break out on her brow. Her lips quivered under his look and she could feel her body wanting to push…push against his hand, have him caress her breast, have his fingers close over her nipple, which throbbed. Then abruptly, cruelly, his hand was gone, his warmth was gone, his scent was gone as he stepped back. Not a shred of evidence that he was as in the same turmoil as she was.

'So don't take too long, Kallie. There won't be a divorce until this marriage is consummated so you see…it's in your hands. You have the power to make this go as quickly or as slowly as you want. In the meantime, I'll enjoy the anticipation.'

Kallie wanted nothing more at that moment than to have the nerve to reach up, pull him back to her and give in. Once they'd slept together she was sure she wouldn't satisfy him…a man with his reputation, used to women like Isabelle Zolanz! One night with Kallie would cure him of whatever madness she was sure was just tied up with his lust for revenge.

He turned and stalked to the door, turning back just as he reached it. 'Dinner will be served at eight.'

She stood for a long time, waiting for her body to cool down. A curt knock came on the door and Kallie steeled herself, expecting to see Alexandros again. But it opened to reveal Thea, who put her bags inside the door. She was almost gone when Kallie called to her. 'Thea…' She walked over when the woman stopped, her heart aching that Thea could be so cold.

'Thea…it's good to see you again.'

The older woman just looked at Kallie, grunted something unintelligible and left.

Kallie went and sat down on the bed. Her head reeled. Little had she known that when Alexandros had stormed out of her life seven years ago she'd be back to face her demons. And how…

CHAPTER EIGHT

'You look tired.'

'Thanks,' Kallie replied dryly, noting that *he* looked vibrant, vital and more alive than anyone she'd ever known. They were sitting at a wrought-iron table, covered with a white linen tablecloth, on the back terrace. The French doors to the salon inside had been thrown open. Thea had insisted on serving dinner out here, more, Kallie was sure, for Alexandros's pleasure than hers. But Kallie had to admit that it was magical. Chinese lanterns threw shapes on the ground at their feet, she could just make out the glimmer of water from the pool on the next level down and the glinting, twinkling lights of Athens and the Acropolis in the distance were mesmerising.

'I'd forgotten how breathtaking this view is.'

'Yes. It is.'

The tension was giving Kallie a headache. Their conversation over dinner had been stilted and forced. And Kallie dreaded to think what Alexandros might expect that night. She stood up, her chair sounding harsh on the stone.

'I'm going to turn in. It's been a long day.' Her voice sounded too forced. He looked up at her and Kallie knew that if he was to stand up and take her in his arms, she'd be lost. He just nodded and she felt an irrational surge of disappointment. She went to walk past him and just when she was nearly clear, he grabbed her wrist in a loose yet firm grip. Her heart skidded to a halt. She looked at him warily, eyes glinting green and blue in the light.

His voice was silky. 'Kallie, that door will be open. Don't forget.'

Kallie jerked her hand out of his grip and fled. As much as she perversely wanted him to make a move, she knew she couldn't. Not yet.

Alexandros swallowed the last of his wine with almost a savage movement. This evening had been purgatory, sitting opposite Kallie with the lanterns and moonlight bathing her skin in a warm milky glow. It had looked so smooth, so silky that it had taken all the strength he'd possessed not to reach out and touch her. But she'd caught him off guard again. Every time he'd moved, she'd flinched slightly and looked at him with those huge wary eyes. Even though he'd seen the blatant desire in their depths.

She'd come down to dinner dressed in loose trousers and a long flowing cardigan, its low neckline hinting at the naked body beneath. Her hair had been soft and loose over her shoulders. Why did he have to desire her so much? It was quite possible that he could have met her with her uncle, not found her attractive and let it go at that. He knew that the lust for revenge had been born out of that fierce desire he'd felt on first sight, before he'd recognised who she was…

The view became a blur. She certainly wasn't like any other woman he knew or had been with. With them things were easy, it was like a dance he knew well. With Kallie… He shook his head abruptly. Enough! It was their common links, shared history, that was all. Being back here in Athens. He hadn't been here for a long time and now to be back here with Kallie, it was only natural his thoughts would turn inward. Making him think about the past and things he hadn't thought of for a long time.

He stood with a brusque movement and finally went inside, doing his best to shut down the wayward thoughts that made him nervous. He wondered if he was a complete fool to let her dictate when she'd be in his bed. He comforted himself with the thought that it wouldn't be long. She had as little desire for this marriage as he did. And apart from that, *their* desire, unchecked, would soon burst into flames.

The following morning when she woke up, Kallie had a quick shower and dressed. Choosing a plain skirt and vest top and sticking her feet into flip-flops, she headed downstairs and found herself in the kitchen. It brought back so many good memories that she was lost in a dream and jumped when Thea surprised her. A terse greeting. Kallie sighed and went into the dining room, as it was obvious she wasn't welcome in the kitchen. When Thea came to clear the plates after breakfast, Kallie asked casually about Alexandros, who she still hadn't seen that morning. Thea told her he'd gone to Athens to his office for the day.

Kallie's insides plummeted. A whole day alone in the villa, being frozen out by Thea. She felt something rise up and told herself fiercely that she wouldn't miss Alexandros's company.

Oh, be honest with yourself. When he's near you your whole body comes to life, your brain clicks into high gear and you've never felt so aware...or stimulated...

With the mocking voice in her head, Kallie explored the Kouros villa from top to bottom again. Although she studiously avoided going anywhere near the patio, as her heart started to thump erratically when she passed near it. She couldn't bear the thought of seeing it again, the place of her original humiliation.

And though she knew she could get a key from Thea and

go next door to see her grandmother's house, she knew it wasn't time. She was feeling far too vulnerable. Afraid of what it might spark off within her, what feelings she might be forced to face.

That evening when Alexandros returned he felt hot and sticky and cross with himself for having gone into Athens. A visit to his mother hadn't helped his mood. She was as cold and wrapped up in herself as ever. He didn't need to remind himself that she hadn't even been bothered coming to the wedding. His own family had been in woefully short supply. After making sure she had everything she needed, he'd left. Which she'd barely noticed.

When he'd been born, as an unplanned late arrival, ten years after the youngest daughter, his parents had only been happy for the fact that they'd finally had a boy, and a proper heir. Their own interests always had been in themselves, not their children, and Alexandros's sisters had all been married by the time he'd been in his early teens. He'd long ago shut himself off from the pain of his family's indifference.

Climbing up the hill to the villa in his four-wheel-drive he found his thoughts straying in an annoyingly familiar direction. Kallie. Wondering what she would have done that day. He'd needed space, had gone into Athens primarily for that…and yet bizarrely he felt slightly guilty. He frowned at his capricious emotions.

It was quiet when he entered, the coolness inside bathing and soothing him. Soothing his frayed edges. He walked from room to room. There was no sign of Thea or Kallie, and he finally descended down the levels until he came out by the pool. At first the setting sun dazzled him and he had to put on his sunglasses, then he saw her. His body tightened and his breathing quickened in an entirely involuntary response. She was dressed in tracksuit bottoms and a tight

vest top and was doing a series of movements facing the
sun. He knew what she was doing, yet even though he knew
it was yoga, it seemed like something more mysterious,
reverential.

Without the cover of layers, he could see her body in all
its supple glory. It wasn't stick thin and muscly, which he
usually associated with the yoga physique, she had curves and
a soft belly and full breasts. Her movements were controlled
and so graceful that it almost hurt to watch. Holding his
breath without even realising, he stared transfixed as she
came to a standing halt and pressed her hands together at the
centre of her chest and bowed her head in the universal
symbol of prayer and thanks. She looked so serene and
peaceful that Alexandros felt a twinge of jealousy. And then
she turned and saw him.

'Oh…'

He could see her chest rise and fall after the exertion and
was glad of the dark glasses that shaded his eyes. That hid
what he knew would be an almost feral gleam, as she brought
that instinct out in him. A need to possess…to devour.

She picked up the towel that she'd been using as a mat and
drew it across her chest as if to try and hide behind it.

'Alexandros.' Her voice came out cool and yet slightly
breathy, making fine hairs stand up all over his body in reaction.

He strolled towards her, hands in pockets, devastating eyes
hidden. How much had he seen? She hated the thought that
he had been witness to what was a very private thing for her.
He was enjoying her discomfort.

His hands, deep in the pockets, stretched the fabric across
his pelvis. Kallie's eyes dropped in a reflex and hurriedly she
lifted them again, her cheeks scorching with mortification
when she registered the bulge.

'Yoga?' He lifted a mocking brow. 'Not something I would
have associated with you—the ultimate party girl.'

'Why?' asked Kallie sweetly, burning up under his shaded look. 'Doesn't it fit with your view of me as a heartless seductress?'

His big body went very still and Kallie almost took a step back. She should have known by now not to provoke him. He stepped very close, but she stood her ground.

An X-rated image raced into his head at that moment and had him clench his jaw in reaction to what it might be like to see Kallie, her strong supple body naked, under his, legs wrapped around his back as he sank in…deeper and deeper…

'Not at all. Quite the contrary, in fact. It's certainly going to make our time in the bedroom more…enjoyable.' His gaze dropped down her body and she knew her nipples had peaked and were pushing against the thin fabric of her top. She clutched the towel even tighter to her body and felt a drop of sweat roll down between her breasts and wondered perversely if he'd seen it.

After long moments Alexandros stepped back and indicated for Kallie to precede him back into the house. Her spine straight, back stiff, she walked in. She fought the urge to run and just then remembered his other comment. She whirled around.

'And what's that supposed to mean—party girl?'

He stopped short, surprised by her question. 'Just that. I looked you up, Kallie. Never out of the society pages. In fact, I'm surprised we haven't bumped into one another long before now as you seem to hit every night spot with alarming regularity.'

Kallie simmered when she thought of the long hours, the back-breaking work she had put in to get her business off the ground. Invariably on those nights that he had talked about, she'd been up the next morning to go back to work at six a.m., and certainly not sleeping off the rigours of a mad night out. Especially when she didn't even drink!

'I'm surprised, Alexandros. For someone with a seemingly insatiable desire to take over the world, that you don't recognise another workaholic when you see one.' She shrugged. 'Think what you will, though, I really couldn't care less.'

Liar…

Her words caught at him, tugged him into a memory from long ago, and he felt an immediate need to justify…something. And how could she claim to be a workaholic? If that work included being out among the B-list and C-list celebrities till dawn every morning? He'd always had a scathing disregard for her profession and only used his own PR in a very calculating way. Unfortunately, the way the media worked today, as he knew all too well, his need for such a company was imperative. He strode on ahead of her, taciturn and dark.

'We're eating out tonight.'

Kallie's rage dissipated like lightning. Her mouth dried up. *And then…?*

'OK,' she blurted out. Anything to avoid being alone with him in the villa, being wound up, suited her just fine. In fact, it'd be easier if she didn't have to look at him at all. She hurried after him. 'You know we don't have to eat out together. If you want, you could go out. I don't mind staying in.'

He ignored her, not even looking back. 'We'll go out in a couple of hours.'

She stuck out her tongue in a ridiculously childish gesture at his back and curiously it actually did make her feel a little better. She followed her autocratic husband into the villa.

Alexandros sat sprawled in a chair in the hall waiting for Kallie to come downstairs that evening. His body had a satisfyingly tired ache. After their little exchange, he'd gone back to the pool and swum lengths to try and forget the fact that he wanted Kallie more than he'd ever wanted another woman. And that he was very much afraid that he'd be the one

The Reader Service — Here's how it works:

BUSINESS REPLY MAIL
FIRST-CLASS MAIL   PERMIT NO. 717   BUFFALO, NY

POSTAGE WILL BE PAID BY ADDRESSEE

**HARLEQUIN READER SERVICE
3010 WALDEN AVE
PO BOX 1867
BUFFALO NY 14240-9952**

NO POSTAGE
NECESSARY
IF MAILED
IN THE
UNITED STATES

to go through the door first. The fact that she could arouse him to the point that he couldn't even control his impulses made him seethe.

She appeared at the top of the stairs at that moment and the mere sight of her made a complete waste of his punishing physical exertion in the pool. As if he'd just received an injection of pure adrenalin, Alexandros shot to his feet. What killed him about watching her come down the stairs was that she wasn't even dressed to impress. She was wearing jeans and a white shirt. Hair loosely tumbled over her shoulders. With barely any make-up and a fresh, light scent pervading the air around her lightly, she came to a halt in front of him. She smiled tightly but even that rocked his foundations.

'Good. I'm glad we're not dressing up.'

He was transfixed by her eyes, her mouth. 'What?'

She indicated his clothes. He was dressed casually like her, in jeans and a shirt. He thought to himself that if he could hardly handle her dressed like this, how would he even begin to control himself around her if she *was* dressed to impress, to seduce? Before she could read anything on his face, he ushered her out and into his vehicle. The ever-present bodyguards followed in another one and Kallie shivered at the knowledge of how important Alexandros was. Somehow, in the intensity of the ongoing battle between them, she'd forgotten that.

She couldn't help the fizz of excitement at the thought of going into the city, she'd always loved the hustle and bustle of Athens. At least, that's what she told herself was causing the fizz of excitement, not the man beside her.

'Where are we going? It's been so long since I've been here I'm sure things have changed quite a bit.'

When Alexandros shot her a quick glance, she saw that he was avoiding her eye. 'There's a new place just opened in Kolonaki I'd like to try out.'

As if he'd even care for her opinion on the matter...

'Is that still *the* exclusive area?' she asked idly, determined not to be bothered by him.

'Yes, but it's fast being taken over by areas like Gazi which are becoming the in place to be.'

Kallie shook her head. 'That place was just full of derelict buildings...don't tell me, some bright spark converted an old industrial works building into some kind of an art space and now it's become a home to all sorts of bohemians and trendy restaurants.'

She saw his mouth quirk, and was transfixed by the sudden lightness that seemed to surround them.

Alexandros was amused at the way she'd assessed the situation in one.

'Yes, those damned bright-spark shipping magnates have a habit of regenerating dead areas.'

Kallie gasped and looked at him. 'You?'

He nodded and shrugged. 'With a few others. Well, it was better than letting it crumble. Now there's galleries, restaurants, clubs...' His mouth tightened for an instant. 'Constantine Stakis had taken control of the area and it took years to clean it up. It was becoming a haven for the black market, cheap, dangerous housing, prostitutes...you name it, he had it there and made a killing from it.'

She turned to face Alexandros fully, unaware of the natural glow on her face that was lit up with sudden enthusiasm. 'Could we go there instead? Please? I'd love to see what you've done to the area. I always thought it had great potential.'

Alexandros felt an uncustomary punch to his gut, a burst of pride. He just answered with a shrug and turned the vehicle in the other direction. It had been so long, if ever, since he'd felt shared pleasure in the accomplishment of something that it kept him silent for the rest of the journey.

CHAPTER NINE

KALLIE loved it. The area he'd invested in had become her dream of what was possible. She turned to look at him outside one tiny gallery that had prints in the window, smiling. Alexandros had the irrational thought, *If she keeps smiling at me like this, I'm not going to last...*

'You've done an amazing job. You must feel so proud to come here and know that you've helped the city in this way.'

His face was closed as he looked down at her and she could see his pulse jump at his temple. She wanted to reach up and touch it but she rapidly wiped the smile off her face. What was wrong with her? A few hours back in Greece and she was already falling back into the hole she'd dug herself seven years ago. She was beyond pathetic and hadn't even learnt one lesson. He had blackmailed her into marriage, for God's sake! Was planning on bedding her in a completely cold-blooded fashion. Her lips clamped together as Alexandros answered her, his eyes, as always, intent, assessing.

'I love it, too. Like you, I always used to see this area as...more than it was.'

Among the myriad, swirling emotions that threatened to rise up and strangle her completely, Kallie had to admit uncomfortably that her first impression that he had sold out to the rat race was undergoing a bit of a bashing. For a long moment they just looked at each other and then it was broken when an amorous couple who weren't looking where they were going bumped into them. Alexandros welcomed it.

'There's a restaurant around the corner. It's owned by a friend, one of the partners who redeveloped the area.'

Only trusting herself to nod, Kallie could feel herself starting to open up, despite her best efforts. She *had* to fight the shifting sands around her feet, around her feelings. She knew that Alexandros had a much more powerful weapon at his disposal for revenge. She knew she could not be hurt the same way again. Because this time she *wouldn't* survive.

Kallie looked around the restaurant again. Holding her back so straight, being on her guard was exhausting. Like her see-sawing emotions. One minute she'd feel herself start to open, like a flower turning towards the sun, the next she'd remember and close up. Alexandros was so much harder to handle when he was… Kallie had been about to say *nice* to herself, but he wasn't even being particularly nice, he was being polite, civil and she was like a pathetic mouse, picking up crumbs.

The dinner had been exquisite, the surroundings beautiful. They'd been treated like royalty since they'd arrived. But this see-sawing wouldn't stop. As if a force bigger than her was playing with her like a puppet on a string. What made it even harder was that their conversation hadn't strayed into any danger areas and she'd found herself genuinely enjoying talking to him. She felt herself relaxing, ever so slightly. Laughing even, albeit briefly, at one point and it felt so good after the weeks of tension and pressure.

Dessert had just been delivered. Kallie took a spoonful of ice cream and savoured the way it slipped down her throat. For some reason she'd never felt the experience of eating ice cream before as *sensual* but, sitting opposite Alexandros, she had to concede that she'd never ever been so aware of everything.

He brought her back to earth and showed her how he patently wasn't half as affected as her when he asked, 'You mentioned that your father took your mother's life in the crash?'

She put down her spoon and nodded warily. *She had?* Why had he remembered that? She looked at him for a long moment, focused on his eyes. There was no apparent malice there.

She shrugged lightly. 'You remember what he was like… always the *bon vivant*.' She avoided his eye now, playing with her spoon. 'After *ya ya* died, things got worse with the company. He never had time to go back to Athens and he just started drinking more and more.'

She sighed deeply, the grief not far from the surface as she remembered. 'That day…that day he'd accepted the fact that he had to get help. But he wanted one more drink…and he wouldn't let Mum drive…' Her mouth thinned when she thought of her father's typical macho Greek bluster. 'So she went, too, not wanting him to be alone.'

She finally lifted slightly defiant eyes to Alexandros and he was surprised. What had he expected? That she'd be looking for sympathy? He found himself responding from somewhere instinctive. 'I'm sorry, Kallie. I had no idea.'

She shrugged again, awkwardly. 'Well, you wouldn't would you…not after…'

'No,' he agreed. They both knew she didn't need to finish that sentence.

Kallie wanted to get the focus off her. 'What about your mother? Why wasn't she at the wedding?'

The change was stunning and immediate. His face shuttered, his eyes black pools. Kallie thought he wasn't going to answer until finally he said, 'She's never been one for travelling. She's happy as long as she knows that Kouros Shipping is making enough money to keep her in comfort.'

His voice was so cold and detached that Kallie sucked in a breath. She wasn't fooled. He spoke as though he didn't care but she could sense his pain, having been through intense grief herself, and could feel it as clear as day in him. But she knew he wouldn't appreciate her sympathy. She couldn't believe the well of emotion that rose up within her, making her want to go and take him in her arms. When she put down the spoon her hand was trembling and it clattered against the plate, making her start.

She excused herself to go to the ladies before he could read something in her expression and only came back when she felt composed. Coffee was waiting for her. She looked over. 'Thanks…but I didn't order coffee…'

'It's on the house…a treat from my friend Theo.'

She shrugged. 'OK…'

A silence stretched between them. Alexandros seemed to be brooding. They'd obviously used up the little conversation they had. Kallie's thoughts strayed as she sipped the coffee. Very soon they'd be back in the villa. Alone. Would he leave the door open tonight? Would he ask her to sleep with him? Would he kiss her into submission? Force her? *He wouldn't have to…*

Kallie's heart speeded up as she took a bigger gulp of coffee. She couldn't look across the table. She took some more coffee. Anything to distract her thoughts. It had a slightly funny taste that made her wrinkle her nose.

Half idly, belying the turmoil of her thoughts, she asked, 'What's in this coffee? It tastes different.'

Alexandros looked over, his hooded eyes making her pulse speed up, *again*.

'Some liqueur, I think the waiter said.'

Immediately Kallie could feel something slam into her. She hadn't touched alcohol in years. *Seven years.* And suddenly the only thing she could smell, or taste, or *feel* with a nauseous swimming in her head was the alcohol. And with shocking vividness, she was back there on the patio, her head swimming, feeling the acute mortification all over again. As if it were yesterday. Terror gripped her, squeezing around her heart, and she lifted a hand to her chest.

It was all hitting her at once. She was in Athens again. Greece. With Alexandros, who was looking over at her. She could see him frowning…was she looking funny? Kallie felt very strange…and she knew that for some reason she'd stopped breathing.

'What is it?' Alexandros's voice came from far away.

'Kallie, answer me…'

Her voice was raspy, she couldn't breathe. 'I don't know… must have been something…'

All she did know with some kind of miraculous self-protecting clarity was that he couldn't know why she was having this reaction. The room was spinning now and she felt herself drooping sideways, unable to sit up. Then she was being lifted up into strong arms, against a firm wall of something…muscle? She didn't care. She felt sick, but safe. Then she blacked out.

She came to in the most horrific, undignified fashion, hunched over a toilet bowl, her whole upper body dripping wet, retching. Alexandros was behind her, holding her hair back as life slammed back into her and she emptied her stomach. Finally it was over. She was shaking all over violently. She felt herself being pulled back up and a wet cloth over her face and neck. It felt wonderful. Then she was sitting on his lap and being held very firmly against a broad chest until the shaking started to subside. She finally managed faintly, 'Where…where are we?'

A rumble came from under her cheek. 'In the staff toilet of the restaurant.'

Kallie closed her eyes and clung to Alexandros. 'Oh, I'm so sorry…'

When she opened them again, she took in the shower and

realised that he must have had to put her underneath it to wake her up somehow. She pulled back.

'I'm so sorry…'

'Don't be. Kallie, what the hell was that?' His voice was harsh. 'For goodness' sake, woman, if you're allergic to liqueur or coffee, why didn't you tell me?'

But I'm not! Or, at least, she hadn't thought she was. But even as Kallie thought about the alcohol in the coffee, she could see the images flood her head again, the acute nausea close behind. She closed her eyes, gripped his shirt and breathed deeply. This was ridiculous. No way could this be affecting her so badly. It had to be the food…or something else. She couldn't still be so tied into what had happened. The thought that she *could* be made something in her head shut down.

She shook her head. 'No, it couldn't be…' *It couldn't be!*

'It must have been something I ate.'

'We had the same thing and I feel fine,' he pointed out grimly.

She was too weak to argue.

He stood, taking her with him, clasping her to his chest. She only saw then that his own hair was plastered to his head, his chest soaking. He'd got into the shower too? He answered her look. 'Well, I could hardly avoid getting wet, too, could I? I couldn't just dump you in there.'

'Sorry,' she said in a small voice. Again.

He elbowed his way out of the room and his friend Theo was there, the owner, looking awful and wringing his hands. 'I am so sorry, Alexandros. I have no idea how this could have happened.'

Kallie gave an involuntary shudder. Alexandros tightened his hold.

'Theo, it's fine. Forget it….we need to leave now, though, we're wet.'

His friend jumped around, clearly upset, and gave them towels. 'Your vehicle is right outside the door here, at the back…'

Kallie couldn't help another wave of mortification. She was sure the great Alexandros Kouros hated this embarrassment. When he climbed into the back of the vehicle, still keeping her tucked into his arms, she resolutely looked out the window, taking her arms away from his neck.

'I'm sorry,' she said stiffly yet again, her whole body rigid. 'I didn't mean to embarrass you in front of your friends…the people in the restaurant…'

Alexandros looked down at the bent head, her hair no less vibrant, even though it was wet. When she'd taken her arms down from his neck, he'd had the urge to bring them back up. And when she'd gone rigid, the loss of her soft curves nestled into him had been almost like a physical pain. And despite what she seemed to think, when she'd almost collapsed, the entire restaurant could have disappeared for all he'd cared. His only concern had been Kallie and getting her to safety. He'd even bellowed out for a doctor but none had been there.

'Don't be stupid, Kallie. We brought you out the back because it was quicker.'

'Oh…'

He took one of the towels and put Kallie away from him slightly, starting to undo her shirt. She slapped at his hand ineffectually. 'What do you think you're doing?'

He pushed her hands out of the way. 'Kallie, you're soaked, so am I. Unless you want to get hypothermia, you have to take off your shirt.'

He'd undone all the buttons and was slipping the shirt from her shoulders before she could do anything.

She let out a strangled whisper. *'The driver!'*

She was now in just her bra and Alexandros was pulling his own sodden shirt off. Totally unashamed, he ignored her concern. He drew her back against his bare chest and wrapped them both in a couple of towels, tucking her arms around his waist. Sensation flooded her belly, her breasts, making them tighten painfully. She bit her lip.

Alexandros looked down briefly and when he caught a glimpse of two perfect creamy half-mounds spilling from her bra, pressed against him, he felt desire rocket straight to his lap.

The inevitable response became more acute. His jaw clenched, the towel dropped slightly. She moved to get comfortable and he gritted out, 'Kallie, stop moving.'

She felt the hard ridge beneath her and heat flooded her body. The trip back up into the hills was excruciating and by the time they got out, Kallie's face was hectic with colour, her eyes so bright they looked feverish.

He carried her up to her room and gently stood her outside her bathroom door. She had pulled the towel tight around her upper body and looked anywhere but at the expanse of bare chest in front of her.

'Do you need help?'

'No,' she said quickly, and qualified it. 'No…thank you. I don't know what I would have done if—'

'You need to get out of those wet things before you get a chill.'

She just nodded and went inside, stripped off and had a hot shower. Putting on a voluminous toweling robe, she emerged to find an empty room. Disappointment gushed through her. Then Thea appeared at the door with a look of concern on her face. Which she quickly masked when she saw Kallie.

She bustled in and got Kallie into bed and Kallie's final thought before she fell into a dreamless sleep was that maybe Thea wasn't as cool towards her after all. Maybe she could try again. She refused to think of the dark angel who had saved her tonight, who had held her with such tenderness. Because it hadn't been. That had been her imagination. He had been functional, that's all.

* * *

When Kallie woke the next morning, her stomach muscles felt tender. She must have sensed something because just as she came fully awake, her door opened. Alexandros. Dressed and looking fresh and bright. Clean shaven. Her belly tightened and she pulled the sheet up around her neck.

He walked in and opened the curtains that covered the French doors leading onto her veranda. He stood looking out for a minute, hands stuck deep in his pockets, and then turned around. 'How are you feeling today?'

'Much better, thank you. I'm—'

He slashed a hand in the air. 'Don't say sorry, Kallie, you couldn't help it. You must have some kind of sensitivity to liqueurs. Maybe the shellfish.'

You mean a sensitivity to the past!

She watched warily as he came close to the bed. He looked so tall and imposing and masculine.

'I'm afraid I have to go to London for a couple of days. One of our ships has had a mutiny of sorts among the crew...' His mouth quirked. 'It would appear that only I can sort it out.'

Kallie could suddenly see very well that he would be a good negotiator. Tough but firm. Despite what had happened between them. With those people he'd have no bitterness. It was only with *her*.

She just nodded. His gaze slanted down at her, unfathomable.

'Don't miss me too much while I'm gone...'

She shook her head. 'I won't.'

But she would. The realisation mocked her.

'Oh, I'm sure you won't, Kallie.' He smiled briefly, tightly.

CHAPTER TEN

As ALEXANDROS drove away from the villa, he had to concede that being married to Kallie so far was nothing like he'd expected. And he had a feeling that things were only going to get more complicated. Again he had that funny sensation the perhaps somewhere along the line he'd made a monumental error of judgment. For the first time in his life, he hadn't bedded a woman he'd desired when *he'd* wanted. But how he wanted her. If she didn't come to him when he got back, her time was up. No more waiting. He'd had enough of her coy looks and game-playing.

Kallie went downstairs after a while and found some breakfast left over in the dining room. Feeling edgy and not wanting to look at why, she stacked the plates and made her way to the kitchen. She had finished washing them and had started putting them away when she heard a sound behind her. Thea stood there with a disgusted look on her face. 'Why do you do this? *Why?* He is not here now. He doesn't need to see you pretend to be something you're not!'

Kallie couldn't take her words in for a moment. Thea looked so hurt, and angry.

'Thea…'

The older woman huffed, ignoring Kallie, banging open

and closing cupboards randomly. Kallie could remember that she'd always done that when she'd got angry or upset when she'd been younger. It had made her laugh and she'd teased Thea about it at one time.

She went up and put her hand on Thea's arm. 'Thea... please. Can we talk?'

Thea finally let Kallie lead her over to the table. But she wouldn't look at her. So Kallie started anyway, and haltingly told Thea exactly what had happened that night. Right up to when Alexandros had thrown the newspaper at her feet the next morning.

She wasn't even really aware she'd stopped until Thea looked at her and said quietly, 'Eleni?'

Kallie nodded silently.

Thea sighed heavily. 'I think I do believe you. I knew that girl was a bad egg—'

Kallie dashed away wetness she hadn't noticed on her cheeks. 'But—'

Thea was indignant. 'Look! Even now you jump to defend her—what is wrong with you? You have to tell Alexandros.'

Kallie shook her head. 'I can't, Thea. I promised I wouldn't and he'll go after *her.*'

Thea snorted. '*Her?* Of course he wouldn't, that's just the problem. It was you he always cared about, not her, that's why she did it, and why he was so angry with you...'

Kallie didn't believe it. He hadn't really cared about her at all, that had been obvious in the way he'd been so quick to judge her.

'Thea, I can't tell him.' Kallie explained about Eleni's fragile mental and physical health.

Thea gave her a withering look. 'Please, that girl is just a manipulator.'

'But, Thea, can't you see? How can I take the risk of telling

Alexandros when he could very well decide to punish her...or her family?'

'That was always your problem, Kallie, you were too nice...and too naïve. It was always you he cared about...that was where the problem started. Eleni was jealous.'

Kallie winced. Was Thea right? Wouldn't he want to punish Eleni? She couldn't take the chance that he wouldn't. Some dark emotion was rearing its ugly head and she didn't want to look at it. No matter what Thea said, she had to protect Eleni.

Thea got up to make them both some coffee and changed it to green tea when she saw how Kallie paled at the smell. Her unconscious concern told Kallie she was on the way to being forgiven. The relief was immense. Thea came back.

'Child, you have no idea what happened to him after that...you think it was just the break-up of the engagement?'

Wasn't that bad enough?

Kallie shrugged awkwardly. 'I know he must have loved her...' Despite what he had told her before.

Thea laughed. 'Love? You can't still be that naïve surely? He didn't love her. He was being forced to marry her by his mother in order to save Kouros Shipping. He had no choice in the matter. When his father died and left him in control, the old cronies didn't have faith in him. They started to sell out, the company came close to bankruptcy. That merger was his only hope.' She looked at Kallie carefully. 'Didn't you know about this?'

Kallie knew she wasn't going to like what she was going to hear, and shook her head. 'No. He only told me a few times that he wasn't sure how he felt about taking over the business...' She smiled tightly. 'He used to tell me that he wanted to do a degree in fine arts.'

That was so far removed from the man today that Kallie couldn't even believe that he had said it once. Thea brought her back to earth with a crash.

'Which you confided in Eleni, and which she obviously then leaked to the papers, along with that photo…'

'Oh, God…' Kallie had never read the whole piece, she'd been too heart-sick.

'Yes. They vilified him, the golden boy of the shipping world who never wanted to go into the business, he wanted to go to art college! With the merger and engagement falling through, the company going down the tubes, Alexandros had to work twenty-four hours a day, seven days a week to bring things back… But he did. And no one would dare remind him of it today.'

Unmistakable pride shone from Thea's face. The past took on a different hue immediately. The person that Alexandros had become when his father had died had been born out of great responsibility and necessity. Not a greedy desire to make money. Kallie felt ill again. She looked at Thea with stricken eyes.

'My parents…they threw him out of the house. I'll never forget it.'

Thea nodded. 'I thought so.' She shook her head at Kallie's look. 'No, he didn't tell me, but I knew something bad had happened over there. He never mentioned your family again. And, in truth, you, your parents, your cousins were all the family he really had.'

Kallie felt numb. More than numb. She'd known they'd always been close, but he'd always seemed so…self-sufficient. He'd always held something back. He'd never talked about his own family. Not really. For the first time she could see how it could have been possible for her parents to judge him so harshly…if they'd felt they hadn't known him that well.

It was so much worse than she'd ever known. 'He must despise me.'

Thea got up to rinse her cup. 'In truth, Kallie, he was too busy to hate anyone. He just got on with it.' She came back and stood in front of her, tipping her face up with an old calloused hand, her eyes dark and bright with emotion. She looked pointedly at the ring on Kallie's finger, the simple platinum band. 'He's married you, Kallie, for a reason…'

Thea was right, but there were two reasons. Revenge and desire. Guilt burned into Kallie like a brand. There was no way she could tell him the truth, because there was no way she could betray Eleni, risk her fragile health. And right now Kallie felt like she didn't even deserve forgiveness. The facts were still the same. If she hadn't gone out there to kiss him that night, when her instinct had warned her against it, none of this would have happened. And she had. So she was the one who had to deal with it.

She had a lot to think about over the next twenty-four hours. She and Thea were tentatively re-establishing their friendship. By the following evening, after dinner and when Thea had gone to bed, Kallie sat up, determined to wait for Alexandros to come home. She wasn't sure what she was going to do, or say. She felt as if a protective layer of skin had been ripped off and she didn't know if she could hide it from him.

It got so late that Kallie felt herself falling asleep. Giving up, she went to bed. She'd see him in the morning, or perhaps he wouldn't be back for another few days. She felt hollow at the thought.

Kallie woke with a start. She'd been having a dream of some sort. Her heart was racing and she felt hot all over. Bleary-eyed, she got out of bed and went into the bathroom to get some water. Everywhere was quiet. She immediately thought of Alexandros. Had he come home? She knew she'd only been asleep at most for a couple of hours. About to go and get back into bed, Kallie stopped and looked at the knob of the adjoining door. In her fanciful imagination, it seemed to glow slightly in the moonlit room. She hadn't pulled the curtains earlier.

She felt herself walking towards the door as though compelled. He probably wouldn't even be there, she assured herself. She touched the knob. Her breath was coming in shallow bursts…and she hadn't even turned it yet! With a disgusted shake of her head at herself, she twisted it and the door fell back towards her, surprising her with how heavy it was.

The room was dark. She crept in. The bed was flat. No one there. In the half-light, like her own room, she could just make out shapes. It was stark and masculine. Fitting for someone like Alexandros. And yet there were paintings on the walls, not abstract, as she would have expected, but small exquisite studies, portraits…landscapes.

She suddenly felt like a voyeur and turned to go back to her own room, and in that very instant the bathroom door on the other side of the room opened, light spilled out and Alexandros walked out, rubbing his hair with a towel, stark naked.

She must have gasped, or something, because he stopped, every line in his body rigid, and looked up, seeing her instantly. He didn't drop the towel, just stood there, unashamed and magnificent. She didn't know how long they stared at each other. She was only aware of the drumbeat of her heart, the way her whole body seemed to be melting, igniting…

'Kallie…'

He was real, wasn't an apparition. Kallie finally moved. She turned and would have run back to her bedroom if she'd had the co-ordination, but she didn't. She stumbled at the door and it slammed shut in her face, keeping her inside the room. She could have stamped her foot in frustration. No doubt he was thinking that she had heard him come back and was fulfilling her wifely duty.

Her hand had gone sweaty in seconds, the knob wouldn't turn and she let out a small whimper of frustration. And then stopped. The carpet had muffled his approach but she could feel body heat behind her and she closed her eyes. And all she could see was *him*. Without even really looking, she'd made an imprint on her retinas of his body and it was all she could see now, every toned, muscled, perfectly formed part of him. Not an ounce of fat, not a blemish on that smooth, olive, silky skin.

Heavy hands dropped to the bare skin of her shoulders and she couldn't repress a shudder of reaction. He turned her to face him and she couldn't resist. She kept her eyes closed, knowing if she moved even slightly that she'd come into contact with that hard body.

'Kallie...' A thread of something laced his voice—was it amusement? Irritation? 'Open your eyes, dammit.'

She opened them. And was surprised to see that the room was lighter than she'd thought, the moonlight stronger. The lean lines of his face were starkly outlined, as was the need in his eyes. She couldn't look down to see if he'd put on the towel, the thought of him *naked* nearly made her legs buckle. That tiny movement had him pull her into him. She felt the towel, but it was a feeble barrier against the hot, hard erection underneath. Her legs were trembling in earnest now, his arms the only thing holding her up.

Her own silky vest and lace panties were no sort of barrier either. She felt the door against her back and his arms slackened, hands coming around her face. He was crowding her, nudging her thighs apart with his own hair-roughened one. Like a deadly inevitability it washed over her. This was it. No going back. This is what she was here for, what had sparked between them when they'd first looked at one another again.

And suddenly it didn't matter right at that moment why she was there, because all Kallie was aware of was his thigh between hers, and how she ached to feel more, experience him fully. She could have tried to run away but she might as well be running from herself. Maybe if he'd come out with clothes on...maybe this heated insanity wouldn't have taken her over body and soul... But to have seen him *naked*...

With a guttural, broken moan of something in Greek, he bent his head and took her mouth in an onslaught so savage, so passionate that Kallie's head almost exploded with the feeling. Electricity coursed through her body. Unable to resist the overwhelming need, she strained to meet him on tiptoe, wrapped her arms around his neck. She ached to be closer and welcomed his thigh between hers, trapping it. She could feel the moist expression of her lust between her thighs, moistening her panties, and moved subtly against him. The pulse between her legs beat for release.

He tore his mouth away and moved it down, trailing kisses along her jaw, down to her neck. Kallie's head fell back and hit the door but she didn't even notice the brief pain. All the muscles in her neck corded as she felt his hand move to cup one silk-covered breast, feeling, caressing through the fabric and then, with his thigh still holding her in place, his mouth touched her, surrounded the distended peak and suckled through the fabric. Her back arched and she could feel herself starting to splinter into tiny pieces. Nothing had ever prepared her for this wealth of feelings and sensations.

Before she could lose it completely he pulled back. Kallie opened glazed eyes and looked into his, which burnt with the glowing embers of his desire. *For her.* It was too huge a moment to take in. All she could do was…experience, feel.

She stretched up and took his face in her hands, bringing it down, and when his mouth touched hers again she sighed with deep satisfaction. Moving her hands down, she revelled in the feel of his skin, his broad shoulders, down over biceps, bunched from holding her waist, spanning it with his hands. Her hands moved all the way down until she came to the towel and she slid them around the back, underneath and snagged it off, her hands running over the taut globes of his bottom.

His big frame shuddered as his erection pressed against her

belly. 'Kallie, Kallie…this is all I've thought about…since seeing you… I want you so much…'

She kissed his neck, his shoulder, the words slipping out easily. She didn't even have to think about them. 'I want you too…'

'Then why did you try to leave?'

She was breathless, half-incoherent. 'I…I didn't know you were here… I didn't want you to think that I was giving in…'

Something about the way she said it, some kind of defiant independence, made her seem unbearably vulnerable. He had to drive it down. 'Well, you're here now. It's too late to go back.'

He lifted her up in a graceful movement and carried her over to the huge bed, laying her down with surprising care. She lay back and watched as he rested on strong arms over her. Like his namesake, one of the fabled Kouros statues. For a split second clarity and sanity rushed in. This man despised her…was bedding her as a form of punishment. Yet how could it feel so good? Going against her instincts to just say nothing, Kallie felt something inexorable rise up within her.

Alexandros felt himself close to exploding with how tightly this woman had him wound. But just then she came up on her elbows, her eyes darkened with passion but glittering with something else. Something he couldn't define.

'Alexandros…how can you…? How can we do this, when you hate me so much?'

CHAPTER ELEVEN

WHAT?

Something in his body went cold. Not his desire. Nothing could put that out now. His thoughts raced even though he didn't want to think. He had to admit that since he'd been gone, he'd found himself thinking of her, the past…wanting to come back to her with a hunger that had to be purely physical. It certainly felt that way now when she lay on his bed, in front of him, eyes darkened, lips plump from his kisses. Anything else, anything more, had to be their history, *that was all.*

That was complicated. But this wasn't. *This* was simple.

When he'd walked out of the shower and seen her there, every muscle had clenched in reaction. She looked like a young goddess. Pale and glowing in the moonlight, her firm breasts upthrust and enticingly visible under her flimsy vest. The shaded darkness that hid her sex a shadowy promise of paradise.

Enough thinking, enough talking!

'No, Kallie.' He was hoarse. 'I don't hate you. I told you once, love is the other side of that. For one, you must have the other. I desire you, I want you…that's all.'

And with a ruthlessness that made him feel on safer ground, he bent over her supine body, found her mouth and took it. Cruelly, to sate his hunger and to ignite hers. She lay rigid at first, as if in rejection of his words, but then slowly he could feel the tremor build until she was his again.

Kallie tried to hang onto his brutal words, tried to keep them in her head so that she'd stay rigid, stiff, unresponsive. But she couldn't. She was too weak. When he'd spoken them, coldness had flooded her, she'd seen the way his eyes had turned calculating. The passion still burned but when forced to think about it, when she'd *forced* him to think about it, his distaste for what he was doing was palpable.

But the wish to hang onto his words was beyond Kallie's weak grasp. At this moment only one thing was clear in her head. Only one thing she wanted more than his forgiveness, more than his acceptance, right now, was *him*.

Tearing his mouth from hers, he pulled her up, her hair tumbling over her shoulders, her long fringe covering her eyes. With one knee on the bed, he lifted her arms and pulled up her top, slipping it over her head. He pressed her back down. She looked away for a second as if she couldn't bring herself to look at him, and he brought her face back with a hand on her jaw. He looked deeply into her aquamarine eyes, that shone dark green now with her arousal.

'Kallie, don't turn away from me, you want me… Say it…'

As if the words were pulled from her. 'I…want you.'

He saw a glistening in her eyes and then she reached up and pulled him down on top of her, her hands on his shoulders, blindly searching for his mouth.

When he pulled back the brightness was gone from her eyes as though he'd imagined it. Length to length they touched. He was careful to keep his full weight off her. One thigh was a possessive heaviness between hers. He skimmed a hand down her chest, fingers circling her breasts. They thrust upwards, two perfect mounds, small pebble-hard tips. He could see her back arch, her stomach contract as his hand closed around one, fingers teasing, pulling at the peak. 'Alexandros…please…'

He bent down and his mouth and tongue laved and suckled. First one breast, then the other. Her hands clutched at his head, directed him, guided him. With his other hand he reached down over the soft mound of her belly, felt the flare of her hips and went under her knickers. The hair was soft and springy. He took her knickers with him and could feel her lift her legs to help him guide them off. They were wet with her arousal and his penis jumped in response. It ached he was so hard and he wanted to thrust in so far and so deep that he'd have immediate release. But he knew that slowly would bring the biggest, sweetest release of all, and she'd made him wait. Now it was her turn.

Pulling her into him, chest to chest with one strong arm, her breasts crushed against him, his hand cupped her bare bottom, the cheeks round and voluptuous. His thigh nudged her legs apart and his hand found its way, from the succulent cheeks, around her silky flank and to the soft curls. Fingers threaded through the softness and then he was stroking back and forth, back and forth. Her mouth was an open gasp that she pressed against his shoulder, teeth biting gently as she fought to keep her moans back.

She threw her leg over his thigh, opening herself up even more, and reached a hand down, searching for and finding his aching erection, which was so hard and full that she opened her eyes wide.

'All for you…' he whispered, and kissed her, his fingers still stroking, finding the small hard nub and relentlessly flicking, circling, before dipping back. Now he was moving three fingers in and out. Her head fell back, she moaned aloud and her hand on his shaft moved up and down, the satin skin slipping over and back. His hand stalled for a second as he had to contain a shudder of pure blinding arousal. She'd almost pushed him over the edge.

'Kallie…'

'Alexandros…'

'Stop…'

'But…I want you…I want more…'

He took his hand away and her sex throbbed. She burned to have him fill her completely. As tangled as everything between them was emotionally, as tangled as their histories were, and as inexperienced as Kallie was, this felt like a dance she'd choreographed a long time ago. She knew exactly what to do. And it felt amazing. Stupendous.

He pressed her down on her back and she felt him shift his weight. She kept her hand on his penis and he came off her slightly and on both arms was poised over her. She arched her back, her hips up towards his, until the head of his penis nudged her entrance, its length in her hand. She'd never felt anything so erotic, never been so focused on one thing, one moment. Here and now. Nothing else mattered. Not the past, not the future.

He was poised to move inside her. Kallie finally took her hand off and arched up even higher. Her hips off the bed, she tried to reach around to his behind but couldn't and put her hands on his waist, feeling the hollowed ridges that delineated the juncture to his thighs. Running soft hands, small fingers up and down. He pulsed and jumped between them.

She bit her lip, about to beg, and then, in one cataclysmic moment, he was *there,* sliding in…pushing into her moist welcoming heat. Her muscles clenched around him, drawing him in, all the way. Until they were completely joined, until she didn't know where he stopped and she began, and when he started to move that she lost all semblance of control and sanity.

Alexandros was in another universe. A place he'd never been. Entering Kallie was like entering a foreign kingdom. Yet somewhere he already *knew.* The way she rose up to meet him, the subtly innocent twitch of her thighs against his that rocked her against him made him press down and into her fully, deeper and deeper. Slowly, enjoying every moment of feeling himself enveloped in her lush warmth, he pulled out and then pushed back in again. And it felt like coming home.

Sweat beaded on his brow, his upper lip. Kallie's head was thrown back and as he thrust in again she looked up, reached hands up to his shoulders, then slid them down, reaching for and finding his buttocks, urging him deeper, longer, stronger, harder. One slim shapely leg caressed up and down the back of his thigh and he was losing it. All will for patience and finesse gone. He needed to have her *now*. Abandoning all control, he went with her urgings, incoherent mumbles, breathy whispers and thrust in, taking her hard and fast.

Her body arched up again, her hips rocked against his and with her breasts crushed against his chest, he felt her come apart in his arms, only managing to hold on himself until the last moment with a control he'd never had to call on before. And only then did he join her in his own blissful, incandescent climax.

Kallie woke with the first tentative light of dawn streaming into the room. She was on her side, facing Alexandros. Just a hair's breadth away from touching, they were so close that if she sucked in a deep breath, her breasts would touch his chest. She looked at his face, which looked so much younger and vulnerable in repose. None of the hard phenomenally successful businessman was in evidence and it reminded her so much of the young man she'd known that a lump formed in her throat. A completely unbidden, monumental wave of tenderness and something else washed over her and she went stiff with instant panic. No, she couldn't—*wouldn't*—allow it to rise. She knew if she did that it would be to admit something that would have the potential to devastate her life even beyond what she already knew to be possible.

She reasoned with herself that it was completely understandable that all these feelings would be emerging. How many people got to realise their dreams, long-held fantasies? And what a dream… She closed her eyes briefly as the memory of what had happened last night washed over her. He had been everything she could have ever fantasised about and then some. A lover beyond compare, a master of the art, more in tune with her body than even she had been. Eliciting a response that made her dizzy with desire all over again. He'd taken her to the brink and past it over and over again. She had been as insatiable as him.

She opened her eyes again and studiously avoided looking down that tempting body stretched alongside her. Thea's words came back into her head like poison. Insidious and spreading throughout her body, tainting what had happened. Things were so much worse than she could have ever imagined. What would his reaction be when he woke up? Perhaps a mocking, triumphant smile? She didn't want to wait and find out, as myriad scenarios flooded her brain, all of them leaving her feeling exposed and far too vulnerable.

She cringed when she thought of the pitiable fight she'd put up. She may as well have just been waiting on his bed, gift-wrapped. *That* finally gave her the impetus to move. With stealthy grace Kallie slid from the bed and paused to pick up her strewn bits of nightwear, a blush staining her cheeks as she did so and quietly let herself out of the room.

When Alexandros woke up, he let himself lie there without opening his eyes for a few moments. He was feeling… replete, complete. For the first time in his life. The memory of Kallie's body under his, so responsive, made a smile curve his lips. *Never* before had he had the experience of feeling like this afterwards. And as he woke a little more, the sated feeling was there but another feeling superseded it, which surprised him with its strength. A hunger. A craving, aching hunger of a body having tasted paradise and wanting more—*now*.

He smiled even wider as he thought of his instruction to his solicitor to have divorce papers ready for after the honeymoon. If he was feeling like this after one night, he anticipated the marriage lasting a little longer than a few weeks. This revenge was definitely sweet.

Where was she anyway? When they'd fallen asleep, exhausted, she'd been tucked into his chest, one lissome leg thrown over his. He stretched out an arm, the smile still on his face, expecting to find a warm, sexy body. Except he didn't. His eyes snapped open, awake immediately. He jerked up. The bed was empty. Sunlight streamed in the window. He looked at the clock.

'Theos!'

He never slept this late. Hadn't slept this late in years. And he'd never woken up after a night spent with a woman in his bed to find her gone. He was *always* the one who woke first, left first. The one in control. He leapt out of the bed and pulled on jeans and a T-shirt. It was only at the door, as he opened it, that he thought of something. A dark scowl marring his face, he quickly checked Kallie's room but it too was empty. His scowl got worse.

With his irritation growing and not really sure why he felt so annoyed, Alexandros came to the kitchen last. Sun was streaming in through the open door that led out to Thea's small patio, where she had her herb garden and a tiny olive grove. He could hear muted voices and the sound of laughter.

Was that Kallie?

He walked to the door and stood stunned at the sight, as a whole other host of reactions settled into his bloodstream on seeing Kallie again. She was dressed in long shorts, a peasant-style vest top, her hair tied back and a bright scarf protecting it from the sun. Bare feet. She and Thea had their heads close together over some pots they were replanting. Since when had Thea and Kallie become friends again? He'd seen the way

Thea had frozen Kallie out and had even felt a little sorry for her. But now…it reminded him so painfully of another time, so long ago that an inarticulate sound made both women start and turn around.

Kallie reacted quickly, her smile fading fast as she took in the dark mood that clung to Alexandros. He looked livid as he glared at her. Thankfully Thea provided a diversion, declaring in a flurry of movement that she would make him some breakfast. Alexandros never took his eyes off Kallie and stopped Thea going back inside with a curt 'No!'

To Kallie he seemed to wrestle with something and then he suddenly smiled at Thea, the mood gone. His smile took her breath away and he looked years younger. Like the young man she'd envisaged while lying beside him that morning. Her heart clenched painfully. She knew she was in serious trouble. He directed his words to Thea but looked at Kallie. 'I'm going to take Kallie out for a drive…would you prepare a picnic, please?'

Thea nodded enthusiastically and chattered on about where they should go. When she went back inside, Alexandros came close to Kallie. She had to tilt her head to look up, the sun harsh in her eyes. The look on his face, his whole demeanour screamed, *You aren't going to escape that easily.*

Kallie gulped. He saw the movement and touched a finger to her throat. 'We'll leave in an hour…'

And he turned and went back inside.

CHAPTER TWELVE

ALEXANDROS said nothing for a while on the drive to wherever he was taking her. Kallie was wary. She'd made her getaway from the bedroom that morning as an act of self-protection. Could he be angry because she hadn't been there when he'd woken up? But surely that's all he'd wanted? Sex. She wouldn't be surprised if he'd expected her to go back to her own room afterwards, to come to him only as some kind of concubine. And then she coloured as she remembered how tired she'd been afterwards, how she hadn't been able to move another muscle...

She looked over. His profile was grim. His jaw stern. She felt like reaching across and kissing that jaw, making him relax, teasing him to a smile. Like the one she'd seen earlier, which had been for Thea, not her. He hated her. She knew he did. Despite what he'd said, he *had* to. She represented such an awful time in his life, when everything had conspired against him and he'd been totally alone, against them all. She had to turn and look away again, feeling a sudden ache in her throat. She flipped her sunglasses down over her eyes so he wouldn't see the brightness.

'I thought we'd go to Kaisariani on Mt. Hymmetos.'

Kallie just nodded, couldn't trust herself to speak.

He flicked her a look because she didn't answer him. 'Kallie, did you hear me?'

It suddenly became too much, she couldn't hold it in any more, not after being so intimate with him last night. She turned in her seat as if galvanised by a bigger force—guilt. It rose up and threatened to strangle her unless she said *something*.

Tears made her voice distorted. 'Alexandros, I had no idea…I swear, I didn't do it…and I didn't know…about the other stuff…the merger…'

She gulped in a heaving breath, the tears running down her cheeks unchecked now. Self-protective arms coming around her belly. Alexandros cursed and swung the vehicle over into a layby. He had to indicate to the bodyguards following that everything was OK.

He turned and snatched Kallie's glasses off, putting his hands on her shoulders. Her face was red, her eyes streaming.

'What the hell are you talking about?'

'Thea… She told me…' Kallie made a huge effort to control herself and wiped the backs of her hands across her face. Alexandros was still just a blur in her vision.

'Thea what?' He was shaking his head, frowning.

A big shuddering breath. 'Thea… We spoke… She told me…what had been happening, what happened after…after…'

His hands tightened on her shoulders so tightly that she grimaced. Then he let her go and sat back. The paroxysm of tears was passing. She could see now, and his eyes were black, unreadable.

'I never read the article, Alexandros. I didn't know, I swear.'

His voice sounded funny and mechanical, as if he was repeating himself to a slow child. 'They printed conversations…private conversations that only *we* had…' His mouth twisted. 'You have no idea how much I regret that now…I *know*, Kallie. The evidence was there on their computer system…it was *your* e-mail, your password. Are you telling me you gave that to someone else?'

A physical pain struck her chest when he spoke about regretting the conversations, stunning her with its force. She had to shake her head miserably. Of course she hadn't *given* anyone her password.

They were back to square one. How had she let herself get this upset, so emotional? All she had to worry about was getting through this…experience in one piece. And when Alexandros had had enough, which she prayed would be soon, he'd let her go. That was the decision she'd come to in her long hours of contemplation the previous day. Why, oh, why did she have to be so impetuous? She may as well declare to him right now that she was very much afraid she was in love with him all over again, that she'd never *stopped* loving him.

And that had to make her the saddest woman in the world. She also knew, much to her dismay, part of the reason she couldn't launch into a proper confession. As much as she was still genuinely scared for Eleni and her family, after being with him last night she was very much afraid that a future, however brief, without him in it scared her even more. Was she really willing to plead guilty in order to snatch whatever this man might offer her? She took her sunglasses and put them back on, covering her eyes again.

A shiver ran through Alexandros as he saw the woman before him morph into some kind of a robot. *Why* was she so insistent on proclaiming her innocence? What was the point? Something struck him. And it seemed to make sense as he witnessed her lightning change. Sympathy. She was looking for a way to get to him…to play him, make him doubt his suspicions. What was she hoping for? A more permanent arrangement? To bring him to the point where he might possibly offer her something more out of the marriage? A heavy weight settled in his chest. She'd made him wait till she came to him, and now, after sleeping with him, she was pretending repentance. Innocence.

He conveniently ignored the voice reminding him that he

had insisted on her coming to him, told himself that she must have assumed their intimacy might have softened him up. How many countless women before her had done it? He crushed the concern, the confusing contradictions that had flooded his head on seeing her tears. She was even buttering up Thea, for goodness' sake!

He leant across and whipped off her sunglasses again. She shrank back, her eyes wary, which he read as calculating. Leaning across, he didn't allow her any escape. 'I don't want to hear you mention the past again. It has no relevance any more.'

Apart from the fact that you used it to get her where you want her...

He brutally crushed every contradiction. For the final time. Enough. And concentrated on the woman in front of him, the ache he could feel building in his groin as he took in the way her chest heaved with her breaths. She was as aware of him, this space around them as he was. She *was* lying, he'd prove it, right now.

'The only thing that matters is *this...*'

Kallie could feel the doorhandle digging into her back. Alexandros came closer and closer. She put up her hands but they only met a wall of hard muscle. And her insides liquefied when she remembered touching it, feeling it last night. His whole body was like a statue brought to vibrant life. He was holding her head in his hands so she couldn't move, and Kallie clamped her mouth shut to deny him access. But instead of the brutal crushing kiss which she'd expected, it was soft, tender. His mouth moving across hers, like a whisper of things to come, an erotic invitation to join him. And, heaven help her, she wanted to, she wanted to so badly. He was relentless, patiently enticing, waiting. She couldn't withstand his sensual onslaught. Like last night, he managed to reduce her entire universe to here and now. Nothing else existed.

When he probed, she sighed, his tongue touched the seam

of her lips and she opened a little more. But still he didn't enter. Her nerve ends tingled, her blood hummed. She lifted her hands to his shoulders, trying to tell him silently that she was giving in, acquiescing…and then she knew exactly what he wanted. Tentatively at first, she darted her tongue forward in an erotically innocent foray, touched his mouth, traced his lips…and then delved in to that dark moistness of his mouth, feeling emboldened and heady when his tongue finally met and tangled with hers.

She felt a hand under her loose top cup one breast, a thumb pad running back and forth over her nipple. Her tongue thrust harder, she arched her back, pressing her breast into his palm. And then, as if a light switch had gone on, he pulled back, put his hands on her shoulders and looked deep into her shocked-glazed eyes.

'See? That's all we need to worry about…for as long as it lasts, we're going to be married.'

He lifted her hand and pressed a searing kiss to her palm. She couldn't move for a long moment as he looked at her. She felt her seat belt digging into her waist—she still had it on! They were at the side of the road with cars whizzing up and down outside.

Kallie shook herself free of his hands and sat up properly, mortified. She was as weak as a kitten where it came to him and she'd helped him achieve his aim. She wouldn't be so silly as to bring up the past again.

'I won't offer you wine…'

Kallie shook her head quickly. Her sunglasses covered her eyes. They had found a secluded glade, just down from the chapel which was higher up on the mountain than the Kaisariani monastery, which dated from the twelfth century. An uneasy truce seemed to have settled on them, and Kallie welcomed it.

Thea had prepared a veritable feast. Pity she'd lost her appetite, thought Kallie, which was very out of character for her. She couldn't stop her mind going back to the previous night. In anticipation of the coming night? And *nights?*

The only time reality had intruded last night, apart from her little outburst, had been when Alexandros had mentioned protection. The first time they hadn't used anything. His look of abject horror when he'd realised, she wouldn't forget in a hurry. She'd told him that she was on the Pill. She knew he'd probably taken that as a sign of promiscuity, in fact it was for her painful and irregular periods. And she reflected then that she'd just recently changed over to a new Pill. Maybe that's what was making her feel so emotional.

'What are you thinking?'

Kallie coloured. 'Nothing.' She grabbed some cheese and bread and searched for something—anything—to say to avoid his gaze, his assessing eyes.

'I was always surprised…'

He lifted a brow.

'Well, not surprised as much as intrigued when I heard of the huge success of Kouros Shipping…' She blushed. 'Even though Thea told me it was touch and go for a while…it's the opposite now.' She shrugged and suddenly wished she hadn't broached the subject. 'You just…you'd always said you didn't think you had the killer instinct…'

She stopped and could see the hole widen at her feet. What was she thinking? She was trying to avoid controversial topics, not bring them up. He'd no doubt be remembering the article, how he'd been made to look weak.

Alexandros was glad of his sunglasses as he watched Kallie squirm. He felt like she'd lifted up a protective layer of skin and looked underneath. He willed down the anger that threatened to rise as he thought of everything he'd been through, which she claimed not to have been aware of. Of course it had brought out the killer instinct, he'd had to fight for his very survival. And he had survived, spectacularly. But for the first time that thought didn't fill him with the satisfaction it normally did. What was this witch doing to him?

'Well,' he drawled, sitting back on one arm, long legs stretched out, 'as you can see, I found it from somewhere.'

He idly picked a grape from the bunch and Kallie flicked him a wary glance.

'Let's talk about you. Your business…it must be hard to keep it going with all that socialising…'

Kallie welcomed his attention being taken off her woeful attempt to be neutral. And registered his obvious attempt to rile her back. She dampened down the irritation and smiled sweetly. 'I just take copious amounts of drugs to keep going— isn't that what all people in PR do?'

He smiled and it nearly threw her off balance. 'I might have thought so before, but with your abstinence and aversion to alcohol I doubt it. I'd hate to see you try anything stronger.'

And then despite himself, he found that he was actually curious. 'Tell me about your job…really, I'd like to know.'

She shrugged, not trusting him. 'It's a job like any other. It's pressured, intense. When I'm working for someone, that's it for two or three months. I always have time to recuperate when it's over. But I do have to be available twenty-four seven.'

He looked at her but she couldn't see his eyes. He nodded. Something about his stillness told Kallie that she'd struck a chord somehow.

'But I can't imagine your kind of pressure. You have millions at stake…hundreds of people to think about, their livelihoods.'

Which was why it must have been so awful for him to have to fight for his company alone…

The gnawing guilt made Kallie falter for a second, and she forced a smile. 'My worst nightmare is a client's function being a disaster or that they might not make the papers…or *make* the papers, whichever they want at the time.'

It always amazed her, how one month one client would be doing everything to keep out of the papers and the next doing everything to get in.

Very quietly, Alexandros said, 'I know.' As if he'd heard her thoughts.

Kallie settled back into a comfortable cross-legged position. 'And as for the parties.' She shrugged and picked at small flowers. 'They're just a part of it. Usually I'm only there for a short time, just to make sure everything is OK, then I leave them to it and read about it the next day, like everyone else.'

'You could have had a bigger business…it's just you and Cécile?'

She nodded and frowned. 'How do you mean?'

'Your shares, of course, the ones you sold off…' His mouth tightened in obvious distaste. 'You didn't think it worth investing in the business? Wanted to spend it all on—?'

Kallie tensed, beyond incensed. Hands in fists by her sides, she spat, 'How dare you? I have worked my fingers to the bone getting that place off the ground. We made best new business through sheer graft. There were times I was so tired I couldn't see straight.'

He sat up and pushed his glasses up onto his head. She'd whipped hers off and cursed now. He'd seen too much, she was getting emotional again. She jumped up.

She could sense him get up behind her and turned back to face him. 'I'm not a bad person, Alexandros. I'm *not.*'

Despite her best efforts, she knew she was close to tears again, and she turned away again. Even though they were in a park in the middle of Athens, the city lay somewhere beneath them, silent. She willed him away, willed him not to touch her, and he must have felt it because he didn't. She found herself speaking quietly, quickly.

'After Mum and Dad died, I had no interest in the business. I never had. You *know* that. Even if you say you didn't. I gave my uncle those shares. I didn't sell them. I couldn't.' She turned around again and as he was closer than she'd anticipated, she backed away another step. 'What kind of person do you think I am?'

Stupid question, Kallie…

He felt at a loss, amazed at her passionate reaction. Her expressive eyes. Shining blue and green. And thought, *The kind of person most of us would be in that situation, who would demand every penny of their inheritance…*

'Kallie—'

'I'd already got a loan and Alexei gave me just enough to subsidise it. That's all. The only thing I regret is that my shares obviously weren't enough to help him turn the business around. If they had been, we mightn't be here now.'

Her words rang with bitterness and Alexandros felt something move in his chest. He couldn't analyse it. One of the biggest accusations he'd made in his own head about her was crumbling. He didn't even question the fact that he believed her. All he knew was that he wanted them to stop fighting, sniping…and do something else.

He pulled her into his arms. She stayed stiff against him. He tipped her chin up with one hand. 'Whatever has happened between us, that was uncalled for. I had no right to assume to know what you did with those shares. And I had no right to assume that you were some vacuous limpet on the social circuit.'

She searched his face, sure he was laughing at her somehow and shocked at this abrupt turnaround. How could he believe her about this but not *that?* He had to be doing it for some reason…she didn't think he meant it for a second.

'Are you making fun of me?'

He shifted his hips slightly and her eyes widened in silent eloquence when she felt what *he* was feeling. He shook his head. 'I've never been more serious in my life. Can we call a truce, Kallie? Make a pact not to talk about the past, just focus on this. And now.'

He was offering her a truce. A space to make things easier. For him? For her, too, she knew, if she accepted it. Although his ruthlessness could not be forgotten. He still had the power to ruin her family if he so wished. He'd keep her until she stopped pleasing him in bed. *Bed*. She felt weak. She'd tasted heaven now. The heaven she had longed for all those years ago. How could she go back? And she knew she wasn't strong enough to give it up. Just yet.

She nodded her head, saw the flare of something in his eyes and closed hers in mute supplication as he bent his head and all that did exist was *now*.

After that tacit agreement to a truce of sorts, the next days of their so-called honeymoon fled. Kallie and Alexandros circled each other warily. Careful of what they said. There seemed to be an unspoken agreement that all they had to focus on was the physical connection. And they couldn't get enough of one another.

The villa became a place outside reality. Kallie knew she was in danger of indulging in a fantasy that somehow this was real. That this existed. As if in some bizarre stroke of fate, her dreams as a seventeen-year-old had come true and she'd got her prince.

But that dream was quashed over and over again as it became all too clear that for Alexandros this was purely physical. Kallie had tried to start countless conversations, trying to get to know him better. Last night, Thea had served dinner on the terrace again. While Kallie had tried to find things to talk about, Alexandros had remained largely mono-syllabic. In desperation at her own increasing sense of hu-miliation and futility, she'd jumped up in agitation.

'This is crazy…why can't you just talk to me? Why can't we have a conversation? Am I so boring—?'

Alexandros had jumped up, too, frightening Kallie with his barely leashed anger and the intensity on his face. He'd taken two quick steps, lifted her into his arms and brought her straight to bed, throwing her down. She'd scrambled backwards.

'You're…an animal,' she'd spluttered in indignation, and had watched with a traitorous and increasing excitement as he'd calmly proceeded to strip off. Completely.

He'd come down beside her, holding her an easy captive with his leanly muscled body, with the desires that made her quiver in his arms, even as she tried to pull away.

'Yes, Kallie. But you want me. That's all. We're not here to talk, or to get to know one another. I know all I need to know.'

And he'd subjected her to such an erotic attack that she'd been hard pushed to remember her own name afterwards, never mind hold a conversation. He'd made his point.

Kallie woke early, her head resting on Alexandros's chest, her leg thrown over his. She just lay there. Immediately awake. Emotion swirled around her head, in her chest, making it tight. She tried to keep her breathing even, closed her eyes tight. The ache built in her throat. She couldn't believe she'd done it again. Or rather, she had to acknowledge, things had never changed. She was still in love with Alexandros. The only thing different to when she'd been a child and a teenager was that back then she hadn't known the depth of that love, how all-permeating it was and how sleeping with him would crack her open and let her taste the extreme despair that would come from loving a man like him. A man beholden to none, least of all *her*.

The past few days he'd been looking at her with that heated gaze, stopping her in her tracks again and again. He'd brutally ignored her wish to talk last night, had effort-lessly made her acquiesce to what he wanted… How could she be so weak? She could see very well what he was doing.

It was tantamount to a kidnapper not calling their victim by their name so they wouldn't identify with the captive.

How could she be in love with someone who was doing that to *her*?

Because she knew him. It was that simple. He was her soul mate. The part of him that she had once known, that he kept from her now, would never be hers. She might be his, but he was not hers. And never would be.

A large hand cupped her jaw, taking her by surprise. She hadn't noticed that he'd woken up. Her eyes stayed shut, the ache clogging her throat. Still no words, not even now…and yet her body was already humming, opening, moistening for his touch. The gratification that only he could bring her.

His hand smoothed its way down her collar-bone to the space between her breasts where her heart was beating steadily, and speeding up when he shifted them subtly and a leg came over hers, nudging them apart. The frisson of awareness, the hunger and need after a night of love-making scared her with its intensity. Today they were going back to Paris. Back to reality, back to the cruel, harsh world of media and photographers and *reminders* that all was not what it seemed.

She turned her head and opened her eyes. Her pain was buried deep and hidden inside her. He pressed a kiss to her lips, long and lingering, drew her up on top of him so that her breasts were crushed to his chest. His hands spanned her waist and moved her up and then down slightly where she could feel the powerful thrust of his erection.

She was already wet, ready for him. She slid her legs on either side of his hips and rocked back gently, coming up slightly, and sucked in a deep breath when she felt him thrust up and into her. Looking deep into his eyes, Kallie could feel the need rise up, the need to speak, to say something. The monumental realisation that she *still* loved him utterly was clawing at her insides to get out, even as he took them both on an ever-increasing spiral towards oblivion.

Approaching her climax, Kallie could feel the words tremble on her lips... She felt desperate but couldn't control it. Not when they were joined, literally. In desperation to avoid the ultimate act of self-destruction, she bent down and pressed her feverish lips against Alexandros's mouth, and her words were stifled as the wave broke over her, as he ruthlessly held her hips and his own release spilled into her body.

With Kallie resting on his chest, their bodies still joined, Alexandros couldn't believe the strength of his climax, every time, with this woman. She gave so freely, so generously. She was so responsive. With one touch...hell, without even a touch, with a *look,* she'd be his. He'd see her whole body start to quiver, like a bow, waiting for his touch. Those huge eyes would follow him, widen as he got closer, pupils dilating, making them look darker. And as he'd bend to kiss her, her mouth would open, soft lips waiting...

But last night...every night...ever since that day in the park, when she'd want to talk, he just couldn't. Something shut down inside him. He didn't want to. He wasn't interested. But even as he told himself that, he knew it was a lie. He knew it and hated it.

When he'd carried Kallie up to the bedroom last night, thrown her on the bed like some Neanderthal, he'd felt like a complete bastard. The truth was, he did want to talk to her. He did want to get to know her better. And that was not a part of the plan. Bed her, get her out of his system. She'd betrayed him before, she could do it again. It had taken a stronger will than he cared to admit to avoid talking to her.

She lifted her head at that moment and something in her eyes caught him. Something he didn't know, didn't recognise. Something he'd never seen in a woman's eyes. And he didn't want to know. He shifted his hips slightly and saw the flare of colour come into her cheeks when she could feel him still inside her, growing hard again. With the same ruthlessness as last night he watched with relief as whatever had been in Kallie's eyes faded, to be replaced by desire…as he took her with him again.

And when they were finished, he extricated himself from her embrace, got out of the bed, and as he went to shower, he coolly informed her that they'd leave in a couple of hours.

Under the spray he rested his hands on the wall, dropped his head and felt the crushing weight of something take residence in his chest. When he came out, Kallie had gone back to her own bedroom and Alexandros wanted to smash his fist into something very hard. He was at war with something… and he was very much afraid it was himself. And that he didn't know the terms of engagement.

CHAPTER THIRTEEN

KALLIE had walked around Alexandros's apartment, which was on the Rue du Faubourg Saint-Honoré. One of the most exclusive addresses in Paris. It was huge. It was her first time there. And now she stood in the main living room with her bags at her feet. When she'd returned home earlier that evening, her small apartment had been mobbed with the paparazzi who'd followed them from the airport. She'd been bombarded with questions. *Why are you here? Why aren't you living with Alexandros? Trouble in paradise already?*

Alexandros, behind her in the car, had stepped out and coolly informed them that they were merely picking up some things and that Kallie *was* moving in with him.

Too shocked to speak outside, she'd rounded on him in her tiny apartment, her voice high with tension. 'Since when was I going to move in with you?'

He'd merely shrugged, looking around with interest, making Kallie frightened. She'd wanted to kick and scream, tell him to get out of her sanctuary. It was too much. Her private space was the only place he *hadn't* invaded completely and now he was here, too, looking around like an inspector. This cool, aloof man scared her. He had the power to make her weak. To break her in two.

He'd fixed her with those eyes. Black and unreadable.

'Kallie, it makes sense. They'll be like dogs with a bone. Do you want that kind of attention? I certainly don't and I'd say your neighbours could do without it as well.'

Guilt had flooded her. A lot of old people lived in her building and she could only imagine what they'd make of having to step over photographers every day. They might even get hurt. But the thought of living with him terrified her. 'But surely it won't last?'

He'd shrugged again and she'd wanted to hit him. 'As long as they think there's a story, they'll hound you here. And by not moving in with me, that's a story.'

She'd closed her eyes briefly. The more time they spent together, the sooner he'd want to get rid of her. Maybe it *was* the best solution.

'I'll only do it out of respect for my area, for this building. I can't afford to be thrown out because I'm causing a disturbance.'

Kallie walked over to the window of his palatial living room now and looked out. They were between the Ritz Hotel and the Jardin des Tuileries. A truly spectacular address. And she couldn't have cared less. She could have been in the gritty suburbs for all she cared, as long as she was away from *him*. She sighed deeply. Because she knew that wasn't true.

Alexandros watched her back from the door. It was ramrod straight, her hands stuck into the back pockets of her jeans. Her cashmere cardigan buttoned down the back, making his fingers itch to go and unbutton it, run his hands around to her front and up to cup her breasts. He could feel their warmth and weight in his hands.

She was getting him hard just looking at her back!

She was the image of simplicity and natural beauty. Her hair was tied back in a ponytail, exposing her neck. He knew without looking that her skin had a glow from the Athenian sun, that more freckles had appeared on her nose. In a rare moment of lightness that had snuck up all too easily, he'd teased her and she'd become embarrassed. And then he'd taken her mind off it by insisting on checking the rest of her body for freckles.

His smile faded when he recalled her reaction to moving in with him. Especially when he hadn't even planned on asking her. He was meant to be saying goodbye, arranging for the divorce, having slaked his lust for this woman. And now she was here, living with him... But right now that lust still held him in its hot grip and he didn't feel like it was ever going to wane. A rebellious feeling rose up. He had her right where he wanted her. He didn't need to look into it any deeper than that.

Like an irritating itch, he remembered following her up to her apartment, which he'd only seen from the door before. He'd been pleasantly surprised by the chic, clean minimalism. The shelves filled with books. It had peace and tranquillity, inherent good taste that called to something inside him.

Kallie had paced up and down, agitated. Alexandros had felt a surge of dissatisfaction. What was so abhorrent about coming to live with him? He knew countless women who'd jump at the chance. He'd suddenly realised that, apart from paying for her tickets to Greece and covering meals out, he hadn't given Kallie any money or any gifts. It felt strange. He had to remind himself that he hadn't wanted to give her anything. And yet, why hadn't she asked? Why hadn't she cajoled something out of him by now? He just couldn't imagine her doing it.

She turned around now and saw him. His breath stopped. Her eyes that looked at him now so gravely were not the eyes of the Isabelle Zolanzes of the world. From what he'd seen in the past couple of weeks, she took too much delight in ordinary things. If he offered her a diamond bracelet right now, she'd probably wonder what he was up to and hand it back. It startled him how clearly he knew this, *felt* this. And how far removed it was from the woman he'd imagined her to be that night at the Ritz Hotel.

And how far removed it was from any woman he'd ever known.

That's why he couldn't trust it. He walked towards her, slowly and with intent. Catching her to him, he could feel that initial rigidity, as if she had to let him know she was fighting this, and as he took her mouth, feeling as though it was the first time again, he triumphed in the way with a little sigh she sank against him and became…his.

'Well, when is she going to be finished?'

'I'm not sure, Mr Kouros. It's a big function and Pierre Baudat has specifically requested that Kallie be here for the whole thing.'

Alexandros muttered something unintelligible and put down the phone. He stood up and strode over to his window, hands stuck deep in his pockets. When his secretary put her head around the door he told her to leave him alone for ten minutes. She scuttled back out.

In the past couple of weeks, since Kallie had moved into his apartment, he could count on his hands the amount of hours they'd spent together. The day after she'd moved in she'd got a contract to organise a last-minute function for one of France's top actor/directors.

Now, much to his chagrin, she was invariably up before him, home after him and so tired when she did get back that she didn't have the energy for much else. He'd actually found himself in the unique situation of living with a woman for the first time, yet *not* having a willing partner waiting for him every evening, and had to acknowledge the fact that she was possibly even busier than he was. This certainly wasn't part of the plan. She'd told him she worked hard but he hadn't expected her to do it while she was with him!

Alexandros frowned. The question niggled again. It had been haunting him for days now. Why didn't he just get the divorce? He'd only needed to get married for the minimum amount of time and that had been well served by now. He didn't need Kallie any more. She'd fulfilled her end of the agreement. *Agreement...don't you mean blackmail?*

He conveniently ignored the ever-present hum of desire in his body that told him exactly why he hadn't arranged for the divorce yet.

They'd exchanged a few terse words the previous evening, when he'd made a comment about how late she'd been working. 'You're not doing this just to avoid me, are you?'

When he'd walked towards her in the kitchen, she'd backed away, making a spike of anger spiral through him.

'Of course not. This is a huge job, Alexandros. I'm doing it because I was offered it, not just to annoy you. If you feel like you're not getting your money's worth then maybe—'

'Kallie...' he'd warned.

She'd swung away, towards the door, and he'd seen her hand in a white-knuckled grip on the handle. He'd wanted to go and prise her fingers free, make her relax...against him.

'Alexandros...unless you're going to take this revenge even further and sabotage my career somehow, then I will be doing this...'

He'd come close, trapping her before she could leave the room, and surprised himself by thinking, *Does she really think I would go that far?*

'Kallie, I have no problem with your work. As long as you're in my bed every night, you can do what you want.'

A dark frown marred his face as he looked unseeingly out the window, still back there with Kallie. With an abrupt movement he picked up his coat, walked out of his office and instructed his bemused secretary to hold all meetings for the rest of the evening. Kallie *was* avoiding him and he was tired of it.

Kallie's feet ached. She had visions of buckets of hot water and Epsom salts. She smiled and greeted the umpteenth person coming in through the heavily decorated damask-covered doors. The function for Pierre Baudat was a celebration of his life's work. A-listers from all over the world were there. This was the biggest event she'd been given so far and she'd been working night and day to get it organised. She hadn't failed to notice how Alexandros's bemusement over recent days had turned to irritation pretty quickly. No doubt, she thought bitterly, this wasn't part of the game plan. A wife who worked.

Well, tough, she told herself. And knew that she'd probably put more hours in than necessary. As avoidance tactics went, she was a master of the game. Extreme self-protection. Keep busy to avoid the pain of seeing Alexandros every day. She was sure it'd only be a matter of time now before she'd receive divorce papers and then she could start to pick up the pieces of her broken heart. Because every minute, every moment spent with Alexandros meant that her heart grew more and more heavy.

Cécile hurried up to her side. 'Kallie, Pierre is looking for you—something about the projector?'

Damn. Kallie's thoughts were pulled back to the evening. That was all she needed now, just when the producer of the latest Oscar-winning best film had arrived. She hurried in to see what the problem was.

Alexandros was tense, could feel it in every muscle. And didn't like it. The usual control he enjoyed seemingly at an ever-increasing distance. The car crawled along the Champs Elysées. He had his driver stop and jumped out. He started to walk to the art museum at the end of the boulevard, and as he walked the bizarre concern rose again, swiftly, like a dark cloud. He saw Kallie's face in his mind's eye. He stopped in his tracks. What if someone gave her something that could spark the same reaction she'd had in the restaurant in Athens?

Alexandros unconsciously speeded up, suddenly imagining Kallie vulnerable, weak, in trouble. He arrived at the door of the function, strode through and was stopped.

He looked down at the young woman who appeared to be in her early twenties, very lusciously half-dressed and looking up at him with big come-hither eyes that did absolutely nothing for him. She was caked in make-up.

'Excuse me?' she asked, fluttering her eyelashes at him.

Excuse me?

He couldn't remember the last time, if there'd ever been one, when he'd been stopped at the door of a party. Suddenly Cécile appeared and flushed prettily, like she normally did. 'Mr Kouros! Odette, this is Kallie's husband. He can come in.'

Odette gave Alexandros a simpering smile. 'So sorry, but we have a strict door policy.'

'No problem.' He'd already forgotten her. Looking at Cécile,' he asked, 'Where is she?'

'Is something wrong, Mr Kouros? You seem a little…'

He forced himself to calm. 'I'd like to see my wife, please.'

'Of course. I'll get her.' Cécile hurried away.

Alexandros finally saw her through the crowd and felt what seemed like a punch in his stomach. She was beautiful. Stunning. Wearing a cream satin dress, it fell Grecian-style to her knees. Off the shoulder on one side and held together on the other by a jewelled clip. Her hair was piled high and a slim golden band held her fringe back. A gold bracelet circled her toned upper arm and golden strappy sandals made him want to walk over, pick her up and carry her far away. She turned her head at that moment, just as Cécile reached her. He couldn't fail to see the shock and surprise register on her face and he didn't like it. They stared at each other for a long moment. Then someone said something to her and she smiled apologetically, indicating that she was busy, and gestured to the bar in the corner.

Alexandros felt a crushing feeling. She was OK. He felt a

little foolish and welcomed the respite for a moment. A short time later, he watched Kallie walk over with the man of the evening, Pierre Baudat. When she came close, he couldn't read the expression on her face and it made him nervous.

'Alexandros, I'd like you to meet Pierre Baudat. Pierre, my husband Alexandros Kouros.'

Kallie felt a bubble of hysteria rise up as she witnessed two very alpha males meeting. Even though Pierre was in his sixties, he was no less virile, exuding charisma. 'Kouros, pleased to meet you. Lovely wife you have here, quite the charmer. Don't know what I would have done without her.'

'I know…' Alexandros battened down his conflicting emotions and smiled lazily at Kallie. She recognised danger in the smile, and then he looked back at Pierre. 'She charmed me into marrying her.'

He could feel Kallie tense beside him and needed to touch her so badly that it was a physical pain and he pulled her into his side. They chatted for a few minutes more and Pierre left, wagging a finger. 'I'm going to need her back, Kouros…she's mine tonight.'

Alexandros couldn't help the reflex he had to smash a fist into the other man's face when he said that.

'Alexandros, you're hurting me.' Kallie pulled free and looked up at him. 'What are you doing here anyway?'

'I…'

What was he doing there? Had he really been afraid that she'd be in trouble? Or what? That she'd be flirting with other men? So far, from what he'd seen, she was working tirelessly, harder than anyone else in the room. An uncomfortable prickling skated over his skin.

Kallie still had butterflies in her tummy, which had sprung to life when she'd seen him across the room. Ridiculous. She'd known him practically all her life, and now she knew him even better. They were lovers. And she desperately wished they weren't. But right at that moment she felt as though she were seventeen all over again. The achingly sweet desire that he would have come like that, to see her, meet her at work because he missed her.

She'd gone through all the reasons as to why he might have come…had even dragged Pierre over to give her some time to collect herself. And now an awful thought struck her. Maybe he was going to serve her with the divorce papers here, now, tonight. She surreptitiously looked around him but couldn't see anything. Just him, leaning back against the glittering bar, nonchalant in his suit and open-necked shirt. Easily the best-looking man in the room.

She remembered his words to Pierre. 'How can you do that, say that?'

'What?'

'Let people think that this is a normal marriage. You said I *charmed* you into marrying you—'

'Kallie.' His face darkened. 'Would you prefer if I tell people how we came to be married? That you betrayed me and I took advantage of meeting you again to take a convenient wife?'

She shook her head miserably. An ache formed in her throat as he put two hands on her arms and pulled her close again.

She hated herself for reacting, even now. Her head felt heavy as she looked up.

He brushed the back of his hand across her cheek. 'We do have a real marriage, Kallie. As real as it can be in this day and age. We have great sex—'

His words tore at her. 'Yes, but that's all. If we didn't, you would have divorced me as soon as you could after the wedding, and I wish you had, believe me.'

Two bright spots had appeared on her cheeks and Alexandros could feel her chest heaving against his.

Kallie couldn't tear her gaze away from his. The room had disappeared, they could have been anywhere. Heat coiled in her belly like a live wire, her breasts tingled and pushed against the fabric of her dress. Alexandros's gaze grew dark and heavy-lidded.

'Just let me go, Alexandros.' *For good!* 'I have to get back to work. I'm busy.'

Alexandros felt off balance again, and felt like a fool for coming when he'd had no good reason. He'd acted on an instinct so strong he hadn't questioned it, and that made him very nervous.

His mouth twisted into a cynical smile. 'This *is* a normal marriage. When we get divorced we'll just be joining the statistics of thousands of others.'

She finally managed to jerk free from his hands and stalked away, determined not to show him how he affected her.

She could feel his eyes bore into her back. Tears threatened, blurring her vision as she walked back through the room, the crowd swallowing her up. Why couldn't he just leave her alone? Let her go? When would he stop desiring her? She bit her lip. That would be long before she stopped desiring him… and she knew she never would.

CHAPTER FOURTEEN

WHEN Kallie arrived back to the apartment that night, she crept in and slipped off her shoes, sagging back against the door with relief. Thank goodness that was over. She felt as if she'd been put through the wringer. She heard a noise and jerked upright, eyes wide, to see Alexandros standing at the door of the living room, in dark slacks, his shirt open at the throat, revealing the bronzed column. Tiredness vanished. Energy pulsed through her body and she felt desire, hot, low and immediate in her belly.

'What are you doing up? It's almost three in the morning...' She couldn't keep the breathy tone out of her voice.

He walked slowly towards her. 'I kept you some dinner.'

She gaped. 'You made dinner?'

He kept coming. She couldn't go anywhere, her back was to the door. Emotionally and physically. All she knew was that the man she *loved* was here, with her now, and she felt so weakly happy she could have burst. It must be the tiredness, she reassured herself, even though that had fled like a cowardly traitor.

He was now so close that she could feel his body heat, smell his particular scent, a hint of musk and citrus. Nothing cloying or artificial. All male, all him.

'Are you hungry?'

His arms came up on either side of her head. She looked up at him mutely and shook her head, thinking to herself, Only for you.

One hand came down and cupped her shoulder, feeling the smooth satin skin. 'The moment I saw you in this dress I wanted to do this…'

'What's that?'

'Take you out of it…'

'Oh…'

He bent his head, but didn't take her mouth. He pressed his lips to her shoulder, kissing, smoothing, his tongue flicking out to taste. Teeth nipping gently. A tiny shudder went through her. He turned his attention to the jewelled clip and with smooth finesse flicked it open. The dress fell down under its own weight, baring her lace-covered breasts to his hungry gaze, the nipples hard and pouting for his attention. When his mouth closed over one through the sheer material, Kallie sagged back even more, an electric wire of sensation connecting to her groin, making her breathe harshly. An unstoppable force was building up, an urgency that only this man could assuage.

She pulled his head back up and clasped it in her hands, kissing him deeply. Her tongue making a sensual foray, searching for his…tangling in a heated dance. The sense of urgency drove her. She blindly searched for buttons, popping them open with scant regard for care, wanting to feel his broad chest, the smooth skin, the light smattering of hair which led in a silky line all the way down to his trousers. Her hand traced this line as they kissed. Her fingers met the buckle and all without looking, or thinking, only feeling, she opened the buckle, then his trousers and slid her hands around and under, reaching around to pull him towards her and caress his bottom.

He groaned against her mouth, 'Kallie, Kallie…'

She whispered against his mouth, 'I want you, Alexandros…'

Here, like this, when nothing existed but the heat between them, she could be honest. Indulge her weakness.

Taking her mouth again with a fevered urgency that made her exultant, Kallie felt him reach under her dress, pulling it up, fingers finding the sides of her panties and sliding them down over her hips. She helped when they fell and stepped out of them. And in turn she pushed down his trousers and briefs, which snagged on his erection for a moment. He kicked his clothes aside impatiently.

She tore her mouth away from his and reached for him, holding him. Alexandros braced two hands on the door behind her. His eyes glittered fiercely as she looked up at him, her hands sliding up and down the shaft.

Two slashes of colour raced across his cheekbones, and she saw him swallow, fight for control. She couldn't help but exult in the power she had over him in these all too brief moments. He stopped her hands with one of his.

'Stop…unless you want to make me lose it…'

With easy strength, he lifted her up, her legs automatically coming around his waist, and with her back resting against the door, with one smooth movement he surged up and into her, piercing her moist silken flesh with his. She gripped his neck and stifled her gasp of pure pleasure against his heated skin, against the corded muscles that spoke of his effort to control himself.

Time and time again he thrust up into the heart of her, taking them both on a roller-coaster ride, more intense than ever before. When he thrust upwards for the final time, Kallie's whole body shook with the violence of her orgasm, and shook still as he threw back his head and allowed himself to spill into her, his release unending. It took a long time for the room to right itself or for either of them to have the strength to extricate themselves. Alexandros lowered her gently back down and Kallie's legs couldn't hold her up.

They buckled and she would have fallen if he hadn't caught her and swung her into his arms. She buried her head in his shoulder and he brought her into the bedroom, kicking open the door of the bathroom.

The bath was full, the water lukewarm. Kallie lifted her head in surprise. 'You were going to have a bath?'

He set her down and shook his head, avoiding her eye. 'No. It was for you. I told Cécile to call me when you'd be leaving…' *And the minute she came in the door you fell on her like a lust-crazed teenager.*

Self-derision made his movements jerky, but Kallie was too stunned to notice. He'd done this for her? She could feel the shaking set in again. She just couldn't fathom this…or the strength of her climax, which still left her feeling slightly shell-shocked and sensitive to the touch all over.

She watched as Alexandros briskly turned on the tap, emptying in more hot water. Then he helped her out of her clothes and into the bath, where she sank down into foam and bubbles so exquisite she had to catch her breath.

'I'll go and heat up the dinner.'

She looked up at him. He should have looked ridiculous, standing there naked in nothing but his open shirt…but he didn't. He looked virile and masculine. Her eyes travelled down. Already one part of him was making a comeback. She hurriedly averted her gaze. After the last climax she didn't think she could survive another like it any time soon.

'OK, that'd be lovely, I'm starving now,' she babbled inanely.

He left and Kallie breathed out. And then felt tears threaten. What was wrong with her? And what was wrong with *him?* And how much longer could she endure this exquisite punishment? She let the water calm and soothe her but couldn't relax fully, his behaviour was confusing her. She was out and wrapped in a voluminous toweling robe when he came back to tell her the food was ready.

He'd prepared a delicious meal of pastitsio, a Greek form of lasagne, with lots of crusty bread. Kallie fell on the food, feeling like she hadn't eaten in weeks. Which, she realised, she hadn't really.

He watched her eat, shaking his head. 'You really are unbelievable. Any other woman I know would run screaming into the hills if faced with a plate of food like that, but you can polish it off in minutes.'

Kallie blushed, feeling like the overweight teenager she'd been all over again. He reached across and grabbed her hand. 'It's a good thing, Kallie. Just because you had a little bit of puppy fat growing up…'

She took her hand away and said lightly, 'It must be a refreshing change. You'll be back to watching women chase a lettuce leaf around their plates in no time.'

Before he could say anything else, she took the plates over to the dishwasher. She was unaware of the spasm of emotion that had crossed his face for a split second. He was silent behind her and when she finally turned around, his expression was cool, blank. She felt awkward.

'Thanks for making dinner…'

She quipped lightly, 'If the shipping business fell through in the morning, you'd get a job as a chef no problem. I could even turn it into a reality show…'

Her words fell flat as she watched him come back from a long distance. His eyes focused on her again. 'What did you say?'

She shook her head, 'Nothing, just thanks for dinner. I appreciate it.'

He stood and pulled her close, speaking without thinking. 'You work too hard.'

'This from someone who thinks PR is full of drug-crazed lunatics running around partying?' She wanted to smile teasingly but couldn't. There was a still, heavy energy surrounding them that confused her.

'I can see that I'm just going to have to get—' He broke off suddenly and Kallie saw him go pale. She frowned but he'd gone inwards, disappeared. Shut down. He took her by the hand.

'Let's go to bed.'

With dawn coming up outside the bedroom window, Alexandros slid the robe from Kallie's shoulders. Carefully took the pins and band out of her hair, until it fell around her shoulders. Shrugging off his own top and jeans, naked, he led her over to the bed and curled her back into his front, his strong powerful thighs cupping her bottom. She gave up trying to figure out what he'd been going to say.

For a long time Alexandros's eyes stayed open, looking into the middle distance. He could hear Kallie's breath deepen and feel her curl even closer to his chest. The shock that had rippled through him when he'd realised what he'd been about to say still made him feel queasy. He'd been about to say, without any preamble, without the slightest hint of any warning, *I'm just going to have to get you pregnant...*

The whole night made him feel queasy. The way he'd found himself going to the function...drawn her a bath, *made dinner.* He'd been led by impulse and instinct. And he did not want to look at what might have prompted those instincts or impulses.

He knew what he had to do.

When Kallie woke up it was nearly lunchtime. She didn't panic, she knew she and Cécile had a day off today to recover. Needless to say, the bed was empty beside her. She sank deeper. The glorious feeling of knowing she had finished a job and that it had been well done made her smile. But it wasn't long before her thoughts turned back to Alexandros. She groaned and rolled over, burying her head under a pillow.

After a few minutes she sat up on the edge of the bed and, finding her robe to pull on, stood up. The intense wave of dizziness that struck her made her sit back down again quickly.

What was that? On an instinctive reflex her hand went to her belly. And then, just as quickly as the dizziness had struck, she felt nausea surge, fast and urgent. She just made it to the bathroom in time.

When she had finished retching into the toilet she stood up and washed her face. She had an awful certainty about what was wrong. And she didn't even question that it could be something else. The past few days, the intense tiredness, increased sensitivity, the emotional roller-coaster she seemed to be on…

It must be down to the change in her Pill, just before she'd met Alexandros again. As if moving on autopilot, she showered, got dressed and left the apartment.

Alexandros was curt. 'You have the papers ready?'

'Of course.' His solicitor laughed briefly, his curiosity evident. 'I was expecting you to call a few weeks ago…'

'Yes, well, I'm calling now.'

His solicitor knew better than to test Alexandros's patience. 'Of course. Leave it with me. It'll only take a few days to process the paperwork.'

'Good. I'll be in Athens this weekend if you need me.'

'I don't foresee any problems. This'll be quick and easy.'

Alexandros put down the phone and rested his chin on steepled fingers. *Quick and easy.*

Exactly how he'd envisaged this marriage of convenience and revenge. But it hadn't been quick and easy. For one thing, it had lasted a lot longer than he'd expected, and Kallie had been anything but easy, fighting him every step of the way. But when they didn't fight…he felt his stomach contract in a clutch of something he didn't understand.

That was the problem. His whole life he'd understood. Everything. Understood that he had obligations and responsibilities, that in many respects his life was not his own. Understood that life could be different for others, but not for him. He'd understood that the minute his mother had informed him he had to marry Pia Kyriapolous.

A shudder of revulsion spiralled through him as the memory came back. He shut it down. But despite his best efforts he couldn't shut down where it led him...to that night. The contrast between what he'd seen and then...Kallie.

When he'd felt her soft body against his, her warm sweet mouth pressed against his, it had called to him on a deep level so hidden, so untouched that he hadn't been able to move. He'd been shocked to find himself almost reacting to her untutored caresses, which had been so innocent when compared to what he'd witnessed earlier.

His mouth twisted. Or so he'd thought. He needed to remember that now. To call on that sense of anger, betrayal. In the past few weeks it had faded far too much into the distance, the past...even calling it up was a struggle, as if it was becoming blurred. Kallie Demarchis was dangerous. She had the ability to trick him all over again and he wouldn't let her.

'But why do you want us to go to Athens for the weekend?'

Kallie felt panicky and didn't know why. Well, yes, she knew exactly why. She needed time to think, to be alone, to sort things out. She'd been about to tell Alexandros that she wanted to move back into her apartment, put it to him that it would look better for when he broke the news of the divorce, as if problems were brewing. And *why* hadn't he mentioned a divorce yet? That was a special form of torture in itself, the constant not knowing...

His face was closed, remote, shuttered. A million miles from the Alexandros of last night.

He shrugged. 'You've been working hard, you could do with a break...'

She turned away from him and wrapped her arms around herself. Even though he hadn't mentioned divorce, she knew it hung in the air around them. Was this weekend it? As much as she wanted to bring it up, to be brave enough to confront him about it, especially *now,* she couldn't. And hated herself for it. And he still had the power to do serious damage to her family. But she knew that as reasons went, if she was honest, she hadn't thought about her family much since the day of the wedding.

She turned back. If this was the last time she'd have with him then she'd take it. And when it was over, she'd insist on the divorce. And then think about what she had to do. 'Very well…'

Alexandros shut himself off from the vulnerability in her eyes, flashing blue and green. This weekend in Athens was going to be it. And with it, he'd get her out of his system for good. He should mention the divorce…but for some perverse reason, he didn't want to at that moment.

He smiled. 'Good. We leave in the morning.'

Getting out of the four-wheel-drive at the villa the next day and watching Thea come down the steps made a vivid sense of déjà vu wash over Kallie. She held onto the vehicle door to steady herself. She had felt nauseous again that morning but had managed to make it to the bathroom and avoid Alexandros hearing her. She had to keep her secret. Had to. If he found out before the divorce, he'd insist she stay married to him. She knew him too well now.

At least if they were already divorced, he couldn't march her back up the aisle, and as for her uncle… She could feel the blood leave her face. She couldn't think now about what she'd do if he threatened them again.

Thea came and embraced Kallie, looking at her closely. Kallie felt a quiver of panic. Could Thea see her secret? But the moment was gone as Thea led them inside. This time there were no questions about bedrooms and both their bags were left in his bedroom.

That night Kallie made a pact with herself as she lay in

Alexandros's arms. After the weekend she would do whatever it took to get the divorce. Insist on moving back into her own apartment. He'd have to lock her up if he wanted to stop her. She couldn't take it any more. She felt panicky. She'd even call the police if she had to. She forced herself to be calm, confident that she could make him let her go. So that meant there were two days left, two days sharing Alexandros's bed. Then a lifetime without it.

Sudden desperation made her seek his embrace again, even though they'd only shortly come down from a high plateau. Alexandros was all too eager to comply and for a blissful while Kallie didn't have to think about anything else.

All the following day, Kallie felt like a cat on a hot tin roof. She tried to avoid being anywhere near Alexandros, but in the evening he insisted they go for dinner in Athens. Their conversation was desultory and forced. Kallie miserably had to concede that this was obviously the precursor to the divorce, even though he hadn't said so.

She sipped at coffee. And finally they were ready to go. Silently they made the journey back to the villa. All the way up the hill Kallie could feel something in her stirring, moving. A sense of growing doom, panic. How could she be so complacent? Allow him to bring her here, like some mute sheep. She now had a life growing in her, she wasn't just responsible for herself any more.

By the time they got to the villa she felt jerky and anxious as she followed him inside. Alexandros sensed her mood and turned to her, one step on the bottom of the stairs. Brows drawn together. 'What is it?'

See? Kallie thought, slightly hysterically, I'm not performing exactly how he wants, not following instructions.

'I can't do this any more, Alexandros. You've had your

pound of flesh. I want to go home. Now. And I want us to be divorced as soon as possible.'

He came towards her and she backed away towards the main living room. She put out her hands. 'Stay away, Alexandros. I'm not some puppet on a string. I've had enough.'

She'd had enough? He'd tell her when she'd had enough. That'd be when *he'd* had enough and this weekend was it. No way was she going to deny him this, not when she was patently lying, her whole body reacting and quivering for his touch. The fact that she'd mentioned divorce didn't even impinge on his consciousness. The only thing he could think about was that she was denying herself to him.

She turned before he could reach her and had run across the living room to the patio doors. She opened them and went outside. When he stepped out, the moonlight gave a glow that seemed to circle around her form. The strands of her golden hair glistened. She was backed against the wall, facing him, breathing harshly. His arousal levels skyrocketed. He didn't know what she was up to, or what was going on, but all he did know was that he had to have her. The hunger in his blood obliterated any other concern.

He strode over and caught her to him. 'Kallie, what is wrong with you?'

She shook her head fiercely. 'Don't… Please, Alexandros, you know I can't…can't resist…'

He bent his head and took her mouth. Hauling her even closer. The familiar battle was fought and somewhere he knew he yearned for a time when Kallie would come to him willingly, without having to fight him, even for a moment. But it was lost in the whirlwind of passion that took them over.

It was only after a long moment, when he pulled back and looked down, that he became aware of his surroundings, where they were. It touched something deep inside him.

Primeval…visceral and extreme. Something he had to lash out against instinctively. So many threads in his head… tangled and knotted, and in the middle of it all, this woman. Kallie. History was being repeated and she *had* to know what she was doing to him. He cupped her jaw and laughed softly into her face.

'Very good. I didn't even notice where we were.'

She was leaning back against the wall, hands against his chest, her pelvis tight against his, his arousal insistent against her.

She frowned. He could see a wary light cut through the desire in her eyes. 'What are you talking about?'

He turned her chin with his thumb and forefinger.

Kallie felt shock rush through her entire body when Alexandros turned her head and she saw what he wanted her to see. Where she'd unwittingly led them. To the patio. There was the tree. The place where she had come to find him seven years ago. The place of her youthful folly and utter humiliation. The pain came back so intensely she felt faint, then for a moment she just felt still. Incredibly calm.

And then the reaction set in. The same one that had hit her that night in the restaurant. Her tongue felt heavy, the clamminess, nausea and that awful tightening in her chest.

CHAPTER FIFTEEN

KALLIE was struggling to breathe through the intense pain. 'I can't… Alex… I can't breathe…can't move…'

For a moment when Kallie pushed weakly at Alexandros's chest, he thought she was still fighting him. He looked down. She was pasty. That same colour as the night in the restaurant. Panic slammed into his body, even as he tried to rationalise what could be causing the same reaction.

He lifted her up into his arms and strode through the house, an unbidden and constricting fear making him feel uncoordinated. He bellowed for Thea and when she appeared at the top of the stairs he instructed her to call the doctor.

After Kallie had thrown up, he brought her over to the bed and sat there, cradling her in his lap, until the intense, violent shaking calmed somewhat, until the storm had passed and she could breathe again. She was so limp that he felt a shard of ice slice through his chest. He was about to shout for Thea again when the doctor appeared at the door. The relief he felt was intense.

He paced up and down outside while the doctor examined Kallie. Thea was wringing her hands. Finally the doctor came out and told Thea to make Kallie a hot, sweet cup of tea. Thea left. Alexandros looked at the doctor, barely able to stay civil.

'Well?'

The doctor took off his glasses and put them away. He looked at Alexandros, and led him away from the door. 'From what I can see, and I've given her a thorough check-up, your wife has just suffered a severe panic attack. They're not serious but can be very frightening to the person undergoing it, and to the people with them. The common symptoms are shortness of breath, rising fear, shaking, nausea, feeling like they can't breathe, intense chest pain... She has all those— a classic case.'

Alexandros reeled. A panic attack?

'It happened out on the patio...is there any reason why it might have happened there?'

Alexandros felt a grim suspicion settle into him. 'Maybe... I'm not sure.'

The doctor continued, 'She told me the same thing happened one night when she had alcohol—she said until then she hadn't had a drink since she was in her teens. It's extreme but possible she could have reacted like that. It would seem to me that it's all linked. Something happened and ever since then something triggers the reaction. It's a lot more common than you'd think...' The doctor frowned slightly and shrugged. 'Only she knows the answer.'

Alexandros was grim, things that he didn't want to face becoming illuminated, begging for his attention. 'Thank you for coming at such short notice.'

The doctor shrugged. 'No problem. Any time.'

As he watched the doctor walk away, Alexandros couldn't halt the image coming into his head of Kallie that night, aged seventeen, taking the bottle of ouzo out of his hands and drinking. Yet she'd never touched a drop since he'd seen her again, except that night at the restaurant. If the doctor was right and she'd stopped drinking years ago... He rubbed a weary hand over his face.

Thea came back up and he took the cup of tea she'd

prepared, bringing it into the bedroom. Kallie looked at him from under the covers with big scared eyes. He made her drink the tea and watched as the colour came back into her face.

'Alexandros…' she said finally.

'Shh.' He put a finger to her lips. 'We'll talk tomorrow. Get some rest.'

They had a lot to talk about. He left the room only when she fell asleep, then he went back downstairs to the patio. He didn't sleep that night.

And very early he got into his vehicle and left the villa.

Kallie woke and sank back against the pillows, groaning. She couldn't believe she'd had that reaction again. And could it really just have been a panic attack, as the doctor had suggested? Yet it seemed to make sense, as she remembered her shock on realising where they were last night.

Could it really be because of that night? Could she have been so upset—and hurt—by what had happened that she'd somehow, in her head, placed her fears and guilt onto something random like alcohol that night in the restaurant? Used it as a trigger? How else would she have had exactly the same reaction just from being on the patio?

She felt a weight lift off her shoulders, even as she felt absurdly embarrassed and mortified. What must Alexandros think? A hysterical female. She swung out of bed, relieved not to feel the familiar morning nausea. She cringed again. He'd already witnessed her emptying the contents of her stomach into a toilet bowl. Not exactly the most romantic thing in the world. But, then, what did romance have to do with any of this anyway?

She got dressed into casual trousers and a sweater, tied her hair back and went downstairs with a leaden feeling in her chest. If anything was likely to make Alexandros run to arrange a divorce, this was it. He'd go back into the smooth, coiffed arms of Isabelle Zolanz in a heartbeat rather than watch Kallie throw up again. She didn't even have the energy to castigate herself for that thought not making her happy.

Thea met her and Kallie gave up silent thanks that they were friends again. She couldn't have borne Thea's condemnation any more. Thea fussed around Kallie and made her breakfast, sitting down beside her at the kitchen table where Kallie had insisted on eating.

'When are you going to tell him?'

Kallie nearly choked on her toast. 'Excuse me?'

Thea looked stern. 'You know very well what I'm talking about…'

Kallie's stomach fell and she said brightly, 'Oh, that? It was just a panic attack, can you believe that? I'm fine now. The doctor even said that once you know what it is, it can stop happening.'

Thea snorted. 'Doctors! What do they know? I could have told you weeks ago what that was if I'd known what was happening. I'm not talking about that, and you won't have one of them again, Kallie. You know what I'm talking about.' And she placed her hand on Kallie's belly.

So she had known…

Kallie went pink and shrugged awkwardly, too bemused to even be surprised at Thea's intuition. 'I don't know, Thea. I don't know that I can…until…until…'

Just then the main door slammed. Alexandros. Kallie tensed. Thea stood up and looked at her. 'You have to tell him. Everything. Now.'

Kallie got up and walked up into the hall from the kitchen. Alexandros was coming down the stairs.

'I was looking for you…'

She nodded jerkily. 'I think we need to talk.'

'Yes.' He was grim. 'We do.'

This is it. He's going to tell me about the divorce and I know I should tell him about the pregnancy now but if I do...

'Kallie?' He was looking at her intently.

She faced him squarely and drew up reserves of strength from somewhere.

'Yes?'

'Let's sit down.'

He took her hand and led her over to the sofa, sitting down beside her. Putting a little distance between them.

Oh, God, he's going to be nice about it... This is so much worse...

Kallie felt bile rise and had to take deep breaths to will it down.

'Kallie. The doctor told me what he thinks happened last night, that it was some form of a panic attack...'

The abject and pitiful relief that flooded Kallie when he didn't mention divorce straight off made her feel like laughing out loud. She nodded her head and focused on his face. His strong, hard-boned face. Lovingly took in every feature as if she had to imprint it on her memory.

'Last night...you were thinking about what happened seven years ago, weren't you?'

She stopped breathing and started again painfully. His hand tightened on hers. Eventually she nodded. Something intense flashed across his face but then it was gone.

'Kallie, I've been thinking. A lot. I suspect that your reaction in the restaurant came from what happened that night, too, that somehow the alcohol triggered it, especially after not drinking for so long...'

How could he intuit what she'd only just figured out for herself? Her mouth opened. 'The doctor... But how...?'

'Because I know you now, Kallie.' He gave a small smile. 'I knew you then, too, and I think that's why I was so shocked when you came on to me...'

Her cheeks went hot with embarrassment. Her voice was strangled. 'I was only seventeen… It was a crush, Alexandros. That's *all*. No hidden agenda. I *was* the same person you knew.' She shrugged, dying somewhere inside at having to explain herself. 'I was just growing up and wanted you to see me…as a grown-up…'

'Kallie, the last time we really would have talked was before my father died…you were fifteen. Can you see what it must have been like for me? To suddenly have you kiss me? Especially when I'd been so distracted, busy. We hadn't seen each other in so long and…I just…I thought you had changed beyond all recognition.'

He drew in a breath. 'But I know you didn't do it, Kallie. When I really thought about it and remembered your reaction that day…when I showed you the paper, it was the first you knew of it, wasn't it?'

She nodded vaguely, couldn't believe what she was hearing.

'And you got so upset when Thea told you what had happened afterwards. You said you hadn't read the article. I just chose not to believe you. It was easier…' *Easier than facing uncomfortable feelings…* But he couldn't get into that yet, they still had more to discuss.

'I think it's time you told me what really happened.'

Kallie took a deep breath and searched his eyes. They were so far off course from where she'd thought they were going that she felt disoriented. She felt the inevitability of the moment. Thea was right. No matter how or why she'd rationalised it to herself…she knew he wouldn't do anything to Eleni. So she told him. Everything, right down to how she'd confided their private conversations to her cousin.

Her eyes beseeched him. 'I trusted her, Alexandros… We told each other everything…' Her mouth twisted. 'At least *I* thought we did.'

And then she told him that she couldn't tell him before now

because she'd promised not to out of concern for Eleni's delicate health. That last piece caused a savage expression to cross Alexandros's face.

He stood abruptly and paced away from Kallie, running a hand through his hair.

'What is it…?' She was hesitant, afraid she'd just imagined his wish to hear her side of things for the first time. Was he going to turn around and laugh? Tell her she was lying again? She could feel herself tensing.

But then he turned back and there was such a bleak look on his suddenly drawn face that she was shocked.

'Kallie…' He stayed on his feet, pacing. 'Something else happened years ago…something I never told you because… so much was going on then…and I think I assumed you knew about it.'

'What?' She was feeling scared.

'Eleni…'

'Eleni…' repeated Kallie blankly.

'A few days before the party…we were in the same night-club in Athens…'

Kallie didn't move. She hadn't known this.

Alexandros grimaced. 'She was dressed up. Make-up, the works. Before I knew it she was coming on to me, trying to kiss me.'

He came back and sat down, taking her hand again but it was cold in his. 'She was like someone deranged, kept going on about my engagement to Pia, and *how* she found out about that I don't even know because it was top secret. She kept insisting that *she* could marry me, that her father could give me the same merger deal…' He shook his head. 'In the end, I had to get her thrown out of the club. And then just a couple of days later when you did almost the same thing… apart from anything else, I assumed it was some campaign by your family to sabotage my engagement.'

He cursed himself for not remembering this before.

Kallie's mind travelled inwards, back. She could see Eleni's face close to hers, the way she'd practically frog-marched Kallie out to the patio. She looked back at Alexandros. It all made sickening sense. Eleni *had* known about the marriage announcement… The magnitude of how little she'd known her own cousin hit her. And how much she'd still kept from her, despite the confession. Petty teenage jealousy and spite had done this. She felt stiff inside. He was shaking his head.

'I can't believe you defended her so staunchly, especially when you knew what she'd done…'

'I'm so sorry, Alexandros. I truly had no idea what her agenda was. She must have been so angry. If I had known about your engagement, there's no way—'

He cupped her cheek lightly, the look in his eyes, his tenderness making something melt inside her. She tried to fight it.

'I know…I know that now.'

'I'm so sorry, Pia was so beautiful…' He *had* to have loved her. Perhaps still…

Something twisted in his face and a hard look came into his eyes, making Kallie shiver inwardly. 'She was *not* beautiful, Kallie. The day before the announcement, I went to her apartment and witnessed something…awful. She was there with a group…' He shook his head. 'Believe me, you don't want to know. My only regret about that marriage falling through was the collapse of the merger…'

The guilt washed through her again. 'If I hadn't followed you that night, tried to kiss you…none of this would have happened. You wouldn't have had to work so hard to rebuild the company, my parents wouldn't have been so cruel.'

She shuddered and wanted to hold a hand up to his cheek. 'When my parents sent you out of the house…' Her voice died away. The tears in her eyes told Alexandros all he needed to know. He lifted her hand, as if he'd somehow known what she wanted to do, and kissed it. Gently. Reverently.

'If you hadn't followed me out there, we wouldn't be sitting here now…'

Kallie's breath stopped. What was going on? He was almost looking at her as if—

'Kallie, I—'

Just then the phone rang in his pocket. Kallie jumped. She'd been close to drowning in Alexandros's eyes, close to saying something, believing something…so close to revealing herself again as she had done before. She pulled back, searching for some distance. Space.

'Shouldn't you get that?'

He looked at her so intently for a second that she felt something alien quiver through her. Could it be *hope?*

He took the phone out and flipped it open. *'Ne?'*

After a quick brief conversation, so quick that Kallie couldn't follow it, he closed the phone again.

'There's something I have to do. But I don't want you to move. Kallie, promise me, just stay here, exactly as you are. I'll be back in half an hour—we've not finished talking yet.'

She nodded slowly and felt something momentous move between them. But she didn't dare try and fathom what it could possibly be.

When he had gone, she stayed on the sofa, exactly where she was. Not moving. *How* had he guessed so much? She didn't even feel relief. She just felt curiously at peace and a bit numb. As if something huge had shifted.

The phone rang shrilly in the hall, making Kallie jump. She left it for a minute, thinking Thea would appear to answer it, but she didn't. Kallie figured she must be out in the garden. She went and picked it up. A curt, officious voice on the other end asked abruptly for Alexandros.

'He's not here. He's gone into Athens.'

'Damn! I tried him on his mobile.'

'Sometimes the signal goes on the way down the hill.'

'Look, it's very important I speak with him.'

Kallie felt a little awkward now. 'Well, I'm his wife. He'll be back—'

The man sounded distracted. 'I'm out of my office. You said you're his wife…so you're Kallie Demarchis?'

'Yes.' She felt a prickle of foreboding come over her skin.

'Well, this involves you, too. I'm sure you know anyway. It's about the divorce. He said he wanted it to happen as soon as possible…'

Kallie nearly dropped the phone. And found herself saying in a thin voice, 'I'm sorry, who did you say you were?'

'I'm his solicitor. Look, I'm sorry to be so rushed, I didn't think I'd have to call. Just tell him to call me on my mobile when he gets back, if he wants this to happen as quickly as he said he did then I need some papers signed immediately. Oh, and, Miss Demarchis?' He didn't wait for a reply. 'You'll probably be hearing from your solicitor next week. Have a nice day.'

CHAPTER SIXTEEN

KALLIE dropped the phone back into its cradle. Thea rounded the corner. 'Did I hear the phone?'

Kallie nodded briefly, didn't look at her except fleetingly. 'Wrong number.'

Thankfully Thea went off again, muttering about her hearing. Without feeling her legs move, Kallie went upstairs to the bedroom and very calmly started to pack her things. Every now and then, as if trying to break into her consciousness, she'd get flashes of pain so intense she had to close her eyes and focus on breathing. She would not let this turn into another panic attack. All she needed was to get away from here. Right now. Before Alexandros came back. She'd get a flight back to Paris. Maybe even get the train to London for a few days, somewhere he wouldn't be able to find her.

She sat on the bed and looked blankly at her packed case. She couldn't believe that she'd come so close to telling him…to almost telling him everything. To think that she'd thought for one second that something momentous had happened downstairs between them. Of course he'd figured it out. He was an intelligent man, and when emotions weren't in the way, he'd been able to see the facts for what they were.

All this showed now was that he wasn't angry any more.

She put a shaking hand on her belly. Thank God she hadn't told him she was pregnant.

The door opened. Alexandros. 'Kallie, why didn't you stay downstairs?'

He came in and answered himself. 'It doesn't matter. I can say what I have to say—'

He stopped abruptly when he saw her face properly. It was white, the freckles standing out starkly against the unnatural hue.

His concern was immediate. He came in further but something held him back from touching her. She was so unnaturally still.

'What is it, Kallie? Did you have another attack? Did you—?'

He broke off as he saw the packed case on the bed behind her, looked around and saw the other case on the floor. He felt cold inside.

'What's going on?'

Kallie shrugged and stood up, forcing him to move back slightly. 'I want to go home, Alexandros. Like I told you last night. I've had enough.'

He gripped her arms. 'Kallie…downstairs just now…' He frowned. 'Why didn't you stay there? What the hell is going on?'

She laughed harshly, and when he looked now her eyes were dead. Dread moved through him.

'Alexandros, you know what happened now. We can both move on.'

Something flashed in her eyes, brief but intense. She quickly masked it but not before he saw it.

'Please.' She tried to pull free of his arms. 'Just let me go.'

'Not until you tell me what's happened. When I left you were sitting on that couch, not moving a muscle.' A different Kallie. With *warm* eyes. Not this cold stranger in front of him.

Kallie quailed under his look. *But if I tell him then he'll know…*

But he'll know anyway, a little voice reasoned, when the solicitor calls back when he doesn't hear from Aexandros. *All you have to do is pass on the message...*

Kallie shrugged again and averted her gaze. 'Your solicitor rang.'

Alexandros was confused. How could that have had *this* effect? Then he closed his eyes and groaned inwardly.

He opened them again and clutched Kallie's arms even harder. 'What did he say?'

She looked back up. 'Just that he wants you to call.'

'I don't believe you.'

Anger rushed through her. She shook in his arms. 'Fine. He said that if you want your quickie divorce then you'll have to sign some papers as soon as you get back.'

Alexandros was very calm, didn't react, apart from a muscle twitching in his jaw.

'And why is this making you so upset, Kallie?'

'It's not,' she denied pathetically, even as she trembled and shook under his hands.

'Isn't this what you want, too? What you begged for last night?'

'Of course it is. There's nothing I want more in the whole world.'

He quirked a brow. 'Really?'

'Yes. Please, Alexandros.' That little flash of something in her eyes caught him again. Giving him hope. Even as she said again, 'Just let me go.'

He let her go and she stumbled back slightly. He opened his hands, palms out, and backed towards the door, closing it.

'What are you doing?' she asked painfully.

'I'll let you go, Kallie. But only when you've heard me out. I'm going to ask you something and if you still want to go after than, *then* I'll let you go...'

He was a huge, steely immovable force. As if she could

even get past him. She just shrugged and sat on the bed behind her, her legs feeling wobbly. Soon, she reassured herself, soon I can go and be on my own.

He surprised her by coming back and kneeling down before her. She went to stand up and his hands on her knees forced her back down.

'Kallie, dammit, stay still. Stop fighting me for one second.'

She opened her mouth and closed it again. And couldn't believe what she was seeing. Alexandros's hands on her knees were shaking—ever so slightly, but definitely shaking. And when he looked up, her breath caught at the nervousness that flashed across his face. *It couldn't be...*

'Kallie, I've never done this before. It's new territory for me and it's taken me a while to figure out what's been happening...'

He looked up, his hands still on her knees, burning her through the fabric.

'Ever since I saw you that night at the Ritz...I wanted you with a passion that I've never felt before. *Before* I realised who you were. And then when you bumped into me and I saw you up close...you took my breath away. You take my breath away every time I look at you, Kallie...'

The way he was looking at her...it couldn't be...he was playing some cruel joke.

'Alexandros—'

He closed his eyes. 'Kallie, I'm in the middle of the hardest thing I've ever done.'

Opening them again, they blazed with something that shut her up. 'Using you, making you marry me were knee-jerk re-actions to the desire that took me over. It just so happened that I did need to marry. But I could have married anyone. I could have got my solicitor to arrange a civil wedding, and got the divorce the following week, protected my fortune. But I didn't. I wanted you. And I had a hold over you.' His mouth twisted. 'Which your uncle unwittingly supplied.'

He shook his head, not taking his eyes off hers. 'From day one you didn't conform to what I thought, what I'd expected. And when we slept together…' Dark colour flooded his cheeks. 'I've never, ever experienced something so intense, and it wasn't just that time, it's every time.'

Kallie blushed.

He looked at her and she could see a glint of something in his eyes, almost defiant, as if he was gathering his strength for something monumental. Determined. She could feel something move through his huge frame as he knelt before her.

'The reason I left just now is because I went to get something. After sitting up all night, thinking, I went into Athens this morning to get this…'

He didn't take his eyes off hers, and reached into his trouser pocket to pull out a small box. He opened it up and Kallie tore her eyes away and looked down. There, nestled in a bed of velvet, was a ring, an aquamarine surrounded by tiny diamonds. It was stunning, taking her breath away and yet so discreet that its simple beauty turned her heart over. She watched with shocked disbelief and bewilderment as he took it out of the box and with a visibly shaking hand placed it at the top of her ring finger.

He looked at her and she could see, feel his chest move as he sucked in a deep breath.

'Kallie Demarchis. Will you marry me?'

Her mouth opened and closed like that of a fish. She could feel the ring slip onto her finger even without him pushing it, as if it belonged. She looked from it to him.

'But…but…'

He looked pale again. 'Kallie, please. Say yes.'

'But you don't… You…hate… You don't love me.'

She was beginning to feel like she was about to hyperventilate. Alexandros pushed her legs apart to come between them, taking her face in his hands. She could already feel her lower body respond to his proximity.

'Did I forget to mention that I love you?'

She couldn't move. She was in shock. His hands were warm and heavy on her face, his eyes intense, on *her.*

'Kallie, I love you.' He kissed her forehead. 'I love you.' He kissed her cheek. 'I love you.' He kissed her other cheek. 'I love you…' He looked into her eyes for an eternity until she could read the truth there. Then he took her lips, her mouth, her soul and kissed her so sweetly, so passionately that she felt drugged. Could she believe? Or was this the ultimate revenge? A cruel play on how she'd offered herself to him…

When he finally pulled back, Kallie opened dazed eyes.

He was intent, his voice hoarse. 'Say something…'

She could feel tears well. And shook her head. 'I don't… How can I believe you? After everything that's happened, you don't…'

She gulped in huge fractured breaths, the magnitude of the moment, the feeling of standing on a precipice too huge. He was asking her to do it again. To hand him her heart. And she really didn't know if she could…

His hand smoothed her face, lovingly tucked her fringe behind one ear.

'I knew I was in trouble when I was running you baths and making you eat at three in the morning. Not to mention following you to work just to *see* you. I was enraged that you were so unavailable. My love…you're just going to have to trust me. I don't want to hurt you. I don't ever want you to be hurt again. Trust me. Please.'

She searched his face, his eyes. Tears slipped down her cheeks. Finally she spoke with a husky catch that made Alexandros feel weak inside. Weak with love for this woman he knelt in front of.

'I fell in love with you a long time ago… When I went

to you that night, I truly believed I loved you with all my heart and soul…'

'And I rejected you.' Alexandros's heart clenched painfully. Had he hurt her so badly that she couldn't love him now?

'Kallie—'

She shook her head. 'Wait.' Her voice was suddenly stronger. Even if this was some kind of cruel punishment, she couldn't deny the truth to him, or herself. She had to trust him.

'I was young, very naïve…but I don't regret it. It was a brave thing to do even if it had drastic consequences.' She took a deep, shaky breath. 'I'd do it again if I had the chance, and I'll do it again now.' She stopped for a long second and then said with simple truth, 'Alexandros, I love you.'

She lifted his hand and kissed the palm. 'I love you.' She drew his head to hers, pressing a kiss to his lips. 'I love you, Alexandros Kouros, and nothing in the world would make me happier than to be your wife…'

His hands went to her waist. She could feel them shaking and it made an exultant force move through her. She had taken the leap. His uncertainty made her ache.

'Are you…? I mean, you're not just saying it? Kallie…'

She nodded. 'I mean it.'

He stood and pulled her up with him, drawing her so tightly into his arms that Kallie never wanted the moment to end. The ring twinkled on her finger and she looked up. 'But…we're already married. How can we…?'

His voice was husky. 'I want us to walk around an altar three times, in a church. To symbolise our journey together, from when we first met to when we will end our days…together.'

She just nodded tearily and reached up again, meeting his hungry mouth with hers.

Much later, when they lay in each other's arms among tousled sheets, Kallie looked at Alexandros. He kissed her and slid a hand over the curve of her hip, across her belly. She stopped his hand and held it there. For a long moment she revelled in the silent communication that flowed between them.

It was time… 'There's something…I have to tell you…'

'What is it?' He shifted slightly so that his hand stayed on her belly, but he came up on one elbow to look down at her.

She opened her mouth and stopped again, suddenly scared that it was too soon, that he wouldn't be ready. That what they had between them was too fragile. She didn't want that love to fade from his eyes.

'Kallie?' He looked worried.

She had to trust again. She took a deep breath. 'I'm… pregnant. I was on the Pill but I changed over just before we met…' She was starting to babble and she knew it. 'That's why…I was so adamant about a divorce last night. I couldn't stand the thought of you tying me to you in a loveless marriage if you found out…'

For a moment he didn't move, and then a surge of something powerful moved through him. His hand tightened on her belly. He looked up for a second and Kallie felt unbelievably nervous. It was too soon, it was too—

He looked back down at her and she could see the glint of tears in his eyes. She looked up with worried ones.

'Are you…? Is it too soon?'

He shook his head, unable to speak for a moment. The thought of Kallie loving him, marrying him had been all he'd thought he could handle, but now *this?*

'Us…' His voice was reverent. 'Having a baby…'

He dipped his head and told her everything she needed to know with his kiss.

EPILOGUE

THE moonlight lit the patio with a magical glow. On a seat with huge cushions, Alexandros kissed Kallie's neck and she leant back against his big body with a blissful sigh.

His hands were around her, on her distended belly. Her hands were over his, their fingers intertwined.

'Anything?' he whispered in her ear.

She shook her head against him. The lights of Athens twinkled in the distance.

'Are you sure?'

She turned sideways in his lap, lacing her hands behind his neck, feeling her belly pressing into him. He pulled her even closer. Her heart was so full of love for him she thought she might burst. And she could see it reflected in his eyes.

'The only thing I'm feeling, Mr Kouros, is your son or daughter playing football in my insides…and how in love with you I am.'

She moved experimentally in his lap and smiled at her husband's low appreciative groan. 'Hmm, and something hard…'

He bent his head to hers and she tingled all over, his lips hovering. Thea came onto the patio at that moment with a squirming body in her arms, a mock angry look on her face.

'A certain someone refuses to go to sleep unless Daddy reads him another story.'

Alexandros groaned and gave Kallie a kiss that promised his swift return. She stood with a bit of effort to let him out of the seat. He took their son Nikos from Thea, holding him high. 'We're going to have to work on your timing, young man.'

'What's timing, Daddy? Night, Mummy!' the little boy called as his father carried him back through the doors.

Kallie blew him a kiss and smiled dryly. She'd said goodnight twice already. She watched her family—*her life*—go back into the house. Placing a hand back on her belly, she walked over to the low wall and took in the magical view. She felt tears slip down her cheeks. But she knew that they were tears of joy…

* * * * *

Turn the page for a sneak preview of
AFTERSHOCK, *a new anthology*
featuring New York Times *bestselling author*
Sharon Sala.

Available October 2008.

n⬛c t u r n e™

Dramatic and sensual tales of paranormal romance.

Chapter 1

October
New York City

Nicole Masters was sitting cross-legged on her sofa while a cold autumn rain peppered the windows of her fourth-floor apartment. She was poking at the ice cream in her bowl and trying not to be in a mood.

Six weeks ago, a simple trip to her neighborhood pharmacy had turned into a nightmare. She'd walked into the middle of a robbery. She never even saw the man who shot her in the head and left her for dead. She'd survived, but some of her senses had not. She was dealing with short-term memory loss and a tendency to stagger. Even though she'd been told the problems were most likely temporary, she waged a daily battle with depression.

Her parents had been killed in a car wreck when she was twenty-one. And except for a few friends—and most recently her boyfriend, Dominic Tucci, who lived in the apartment right above hers, she was alone. Her doctor kept reminding her that she should be grateful to be alive, and on one level she knew he was right. But he wasn't living in her shoes.

If she'd been anywhere else but at that pharmacy when the

robbery happened, she wouldn't have died twice on the way to the hospital. Instead of being grateful that she'd survived, she couldn't stop thinking of what she'd lost.

But that wasn't the end of her troubles. On top of everything else, something strange was happening inside her head. She'd begun to hear odd things: sounds, not voices—at least, she didn't think it was voices. It was more like the distant noise of rapids—a rush of wind and water inside her head that, when it came, blocked out everything around her. It didn't happen often, but when it did, it was frightening, and it was driving her crazy.

The blank moments, which is what she called them, even had a rhythm. First there came that sound, then a cold sweat, then panic with no reason. Part of her feared it was the beginning of an emotional breakdown. And part of her feared it wasn't—that it was going to turn out to be a permanent souvenir of her resurrection.

Frustrated with herself and the situation as it stood, she upped the sound on the TV remote. But instead of *Wheel of Fortune,* an announcer broke in with a special bulletin.

"This just in. Police are on the scene of a kidnapping that occurred only hours ago at The Dakota. Molly Dane, the six-year-old daughter of one of Hollywood's blockbuster stars, Lyla Dane, was taken by force from the family apartment. At this time they have yet to receive a ransom demand. The housekeeper was seriously injured during the abduction, and is, at the present time, in surgery. Police are hoping to be able to talk to her once she regains consciousness. In the meantime, we are going now to a press conference with Lyla Dane."

Horrified, Nicole stilled as the cameras went live to where the actress was speaking before a bank of microphones. The shock and terror in Lyla Dane's voice were physically painful to watch. But even though Nicole kept upping the volume, the sound continued to fade.

Just when she was beginning to think something was wrong with her set, the broadcast suddenly switched from the Dane press conference to what appeared to be footage of the kidnapping, beginning with footage from inside the apartment.

When the front door suddenly flew back against the wall and four men rushed in, Nicole gasped. Horrified, she quickly realized that this must have been caught on a security camera inside the Dane apartment.

As Nicole continued to watch, a small Asian woman, who she guessed was the maid, rushed forward in an effort to keep them out. When one of the men hit her in the face with his gun, Nicole moaned. The violence was too reminiscent of what she'd lived through. Sick to her stomach, she fisted her hands against her belly, wishing it was over, but unable to tear her gaze away.

When the maid dropped to the carpet, the same man followed with a vicious kick to the little woman's midsection that lifted her off the floor.

"Oh, my God," Nicole said. When blood began to pool beneath the maid's head, she started to cry.

As the tape played on, the four men split up in different directions. The camera caught one running down a long marble hallway, then disappearing into a room. Moments later he reappeared, carrying a little girl, who Nicole assumed was Molly Dane. The child was wearing a pair of red pants and a white turtleneck sweater, and her hair was partially blocking her abductor's face as he carried her down the hall. She was kicking and screaming in his arms, and when he slapped her, it elicited an agonized scream that brought the other three running. Nicole watched in horror as one of them ran up and put his hand over Molly's face. Seconds later, she went limp.

One moment they were in the foyer, then they were gone.

Nicole jumped to her feet, then staggered drunkenly. The bowl of ice cream she'd absentmindedly placed in her lap shattered at her feet, splattering glass and melting ice cream everywhere.

The picture on the screen abruptly switched from the kidnapping to what Nicole assumed was a rerun of Lyla Dane's plea for her daughter's safe return, but she was numb.

Before she could think what to do next, the doorbell rang. Startled by the unexpected sound, she shakily swiped at the tears and took a step forward. She didn't feel the glass shards piercing her feet until she took the second step. At that point, sharp pains shot through her foot. She gasped, then looked down in confusion. Her legs looked as if she'd been running through mud, and she was standing in broken glass and ice cream, while a thin ribbon of blood seeped out from beneath her toes.

"Oh, no," Nicole mumbled, then stifled a second moan of pain.

The doorbell rang again. She shivered, then clutched her head in confusion.

"Just a minute!" she yelled, then tried to sidestep the rest of the debris as she hobbled to the door.

When she looked through the peephole in the door, she didn't know whether to be relieved or regretful.

It was Dominic, and as usual, she was a mess.

Nicole smiled a little self-consciously as she opened the door to let him in. "I just don't know what's happening to me. I think I'm losing my mind."

"Hey, don't talk about my woman like that."

Nicole rode the surge of delight his words brought. "So I'm still your woman?"

Dominic lowered his head.

Their lips met.
The kiss proceeded.
Slowly.
Thoroughly.

* * * * *

Be sure to look for the AFTERSHOCK *anthology
next month, as well as other exciting paranormal stories
from Silhouette Nocturne.
Available in October wherever books are sold.*

Silhouette®

SPECIAL EDITION™

FROM *NEW YORK TIMES* BESTSELLING AUTHOR

LINDA LAEL MILLER

A STONE CREEK CHRISTMAS

Veterinarian Olivia O'Ballivan finds the animals in Stone Creek playing Cupid between her and Tanner Quinn. Even Tanner's daughter, Sophie, is eager to play matchmaker. With everyone conspiring against them and the holiday season fast approaching, Tanner and Olivia may just get everything they want for Christmas after all!

Available December 2008
wherever books are sold.

REQUEST YOUR FREE BOOKS!

2 FREE NOVELS PLUS 2 FREE GIFTS!

PASSION GUARANTEED SEDUCTION

YES! Please send me 2 FREE Harlequin Presents® novels and my 2 FREE gifts (gifts are worth about $10). After receiving them, if I don't wish to receive any more books, I can return the shipping statement marked "cancel". If I don't cancel, I will receive 6 brand-new novels every month and be billed just $4.05 per book in the U.S. or $4.74 per book in Canada, plus 25¢ shipping and handling per book and applicable taxes, if any*. That's a savings of close to 15% off the cover price! I understand that accepting the 2 free books and gifts places me under no obligation to buy anything. I can always return a shipment and cancel at any time. Even if I never buy another book, the two free books and gifts are mine to keep forever.

106 HDN ERRW   306 HDN ERRL

Name	(PLEASE PRINT)	
Address		Apt. #
City	State/Prov.	Zip/Postal Code

Signature (if under 18, a parent or guardian must sign)

Mail to the Harlequin Reader Service:
IN U.S.A.: P.O. Box 1867, Buffalo, NY 14240-1867
IN CANADA: P.O. Box 609, Fort Erie, Ontario L2A 5X3

Not valid to current subscribers of Harlequin Presents books.

Want to try two free books from another line?
Call 1-800-873-8635 or visit www.morefreebooks.com.

* Terms and prices subject to change without notice. N.Y. residents add applicable sales tax. Canadian residents will be charged applicable provincial taxes and GST. Offer not valid in Quebec. This offer is limited to one order per household. All orders subject to approval. Credit or debit balances in a customer's account(s) may be offset by any other outstanding balance owed by or to the customer. Please allow 4 to 6 weeks for delivery. Offer available while quantities last.

Your Privacy: Harlequin Books is committed to protecting your privacy. Our Privacy Policy is available online at www.eHarlequin.com or upon request from the Reader Service. From time to time we make our lists of customers available to reputable third parties who may have a product or service of interest to you. If you would prefer we not share your name and address, please check here. ☐

HP08R

MEDITERRANEAN DOCTORS

Demanding, devoted and
drop-dead gorgeous—
These Latin doctors will
make your heart race!

Smolderingly sexy Mediterranean doctors

Saving lives by day…red-hot lovers by night

**Read these four Mediterranean Doctors stories
in this new collection by your favorite authors,
available in Presents EXTRA October 2008:**

THE SICILIAN DOCTOR'S MISTRESS
by SARAH MORGAN

THE ITALIAN COUNT'S BABY
by AMY ANDREWS

SPANISH DOCTOR, PREGNANT NURSE
by CAROL MARINELLI

THE SPANISH DOCTOR'S LOVE-CHILD
by KATE HARDY

HPE1008